ECHOES
Of Journeys Past
By Larry Incollingo
Copyright, 1995
A Reunion Series Book

Published by Reunion Books
3949 Old SR 446
Bloomington, IN 47401

Cover Design and Illustrations
Gerald "Mouse" Strange

Other Books By Larry Incollingo
Laughing All The Way
G'bye My Honey
Precious Rascal
Ol' Sam Payton

See order coupon in back of book to obtain or reserve copies of books.
SEND A GIFT COPY TO A FRIEND

ACKNOWLEDGEMENT

For her trust in me to tell the story exactly as it was told to me, I extend my appreciation and gratitude to Elisabeth Lett Jackson. – LInc.

This book is dedicated to the memory of
W. Carl Jackson, skipper of the ketch CARLA MIA.
– LInc.

"Oh Lord, thy sea is so great and my boat is so small."

Breton fisherman prayer

ECHOES OF JOURNEYS PAST
By Larry Incollingo

Author's Note i

CONTENTS

TITLE	PAGE
Charlie	1
The Bus Driver	15
Lottie Roberts	21
Golden Wedding	25
Only One	29
Marigold	34
The Auction Sign	39
Easter Girl	43
Joseph	53
Flossie	57
Dresden Days	65
Taylor Wilson	69
Craig Peters	73
'Click-Click'	81
William Helms	85
The Kimbrels	90
The Toolmaker	95
Tommy & Lydia	99
The Baxter Place	104
Herle's	108
Bridge To Another Time	118
The Euchre Player	123
The Golden Spur	127
Kelly Reed	132
Blanche Tracy	136
Grandpaw's Treasures	141
Harley & Viola	145
Bit At A Time	150
The Old Man	154
Working On The Railroad	158
Down The Track	158
HullCee's Day	160
No. 72	162
A Friendly Toot	165
'Spotty'	169
The Jackson Odyssey	173

AUTHOR'S NOTE

Journey suggests a physical traveling from one place to another, as indeed was "The Jackson Odyssey" featured in this book; a sea voyage from the United States to Ireland.

Figuratively *journey* can mean a passage through life, and in that respect we are all voyagers on the sea of life. Our passages may be brief and happy, or long and sad, but in every case not without meaning. And we hear their echoes, all of us, whether they be the echoes of our own journeys past or those of our ancestors, loved ones or friends. We hear them every day of our lives in our genes, in falling leaves, in pictures seen, in books read and in words spoken.

Echoes of Journeys Past, then, is just that kind of book, a recollection of life's journeys, some happy, some not so happy, but not a single one without meaning.

– Larry Incollingo, May 19, 1995

SEND A GIFT COPY TO A FRIEND
(See Coupon In Back Of Book)

CHARLIE

When vivid yellow daffodils trumpeted the coming of spring to Orange County, Indiana, you could safely bet a packet of your favorite garden seed that Charlie Ragsdale had departed his winter quarters down in Florida and was on his way home to Orleans.

A native countian, Charlie was born and reared at Orangeville. He worked a large farm there until after his retirement, when he took up residence in Orleans. It was then that he also became a full-scale member of the Hard of Hearing Gang, a collection of over – and ought to have been chased over – the hill residents, who gathered almost daily in Elmo Wolfe's Barber Shop.

It was an exclusive group, depending on one's own personal view. Elmo, who was not impaired, nor quite old enough, did not qualify for membership. But by virtue of his commercial real estate holding on the main drag of the small town, and his tonsorial talents, he was granted the status of associate member. There were a few others. Although no one ever put it in writing, I liked to think of myself as also having possessed such a connection to that bunch.

There were no dues, as such. To remain a member in good standing one needed only to stay alive long enough to attend the next gathering, and to be a fairly able bull-thrower. And, of course, to willingly take an occasional turn at throwing some.

CHARLIE RAGSDALE
At Elmo's Barber Shop

By special arrangement that right was extended to associate members, which gave Elmo an opportunity to throw a little bull himself.

When such sessions were in progress it was not unusual to hear a gang member shout, "I can't hear you!" Which gave the organization its name. At the sound of that declaration someone was bound to ask, "What's The Matter, Can't You Hear?" Which was the second choice when the club name was chosen. In third place was, "I Can Hear. You Just Can't Talk Club." Of course there's always a funny man around, and he suggested the name "They Hear What They Want To Hear Gang."

Charlie was one of the more eloquent and loveable members of the Hard of Hearing Gang. Whether he was making the jokes or someone was joshing him, he seemed to be just the catharsis everyone needed. Moved by his sense of humor, someone once likened him to a dose of sulphur and molasses for the mind.

"When we lived at Orangeville," I remember him commenting on that springtime home-remedy cleansing laxative one day at Elmo's, "we were so poor my parents couldn't afford to buy sulphur and molasses. So in the spring my mother would sit us on the pot and tell us ghost stories."

He said one morning of his departure from Orangeville, "They ran me out. It was too small a place, anyway. It was so small they didn't even have a village idiot, and the rest of us had to take turns at being one. Now Orleans is blessed with me."

On a couple of his winter visits to Florida Charlie had to go to the hospital, both times at great expense. Taking a liberty allowed associate members, Elmo one day made the following observation about that costly expense: "Charlie," he said, "sent a couple of doctors to the Bahamas from there."

Apparently pleased to have been of some help to his fellow man, Charlie nodded and smiled. He was also pleased that surgery had relieved a clogged neck vein that had caused him to have three minor strokes that were the cause of his hospitalizations. The problem vein was replaced with a healthy one taken from his right ankle. Two days after that surgery he was out of the hospital.

"You'd think he'd have a pain in the neck," Elmo scoffed. "But his ankle hurts."

"I couldn't figure it out," Charlie smiled. "When I woke up after the operation I couldn't figure out why my ankle hurt."

Neither the surgery nor the shoulder he fractured in a fall sometime afterward had affected his golf game.

"It's as good as it ever was," he said one day after his latest return from Florida.

"What is it?" I asked.

"I'd rather not say," he replied.

"Sometimes he'll break a hundred," Elmo taunted, adding, "Harold Tritle says Charlie swings like an old beer sign."

With those jibes reverberating inside the plastic gadget in his ear, Charlie, surprisingly, was still able to hear me ask how it felt to be back in Orleans. His eyes sparkled as they quickly made the circuit of the Hard of Hearing Gang members gathered in Elmo's, and he answered with his quick smile, "At my age, it's good to be anyplace."

It was not unusual that at this time Elmo should be having a run on baldies and near-baldies. To torment them, Elmo produced a newspaper clip of an Ann Landers column in which a sixty-seven year old baldie asked why he, with little or no hair, should have to pay the same price for a haircut as a "mophead."

Miss Landers replied that barbers do not set prices according to the amount of hair a person has, but for a service rendered.

Trying to be helpful, gang member Bruce Pickens offered his explanation: "A barber has to hunt down what little hair a baldheaded man has before he can cut it, and it takes a long time."

Elmo agreed. "I'll cut more hair off a baldheaded man than I will off most young fellows who have long hair. They usually just want the ends trimmed," he said.

"Nah," another member of the gang growled. "When you get bald you get rooked."

"I hear that at least once a day," said Elmo. "But this one customer who is getting bald doesn't complain. He sees what's happening on the top of his head in a different light. He says, 'The Lord made me one pretty face, and now he's clearing ground to make me another.'"

Ralph Pate, on whose head the Lord also was busy, was responsible for the Ann Landers column being in Elmo's. He carried it in one day in an attempt to bolster his complaint on the subject.

"I don't let that bother me," Elmo went on to say. "And," he looked around at the sober faces surrounding his workplace as though he was looking for confirmation, "it's all in fun anyway."

At the rate of once a day, Elmo, by this time, had heard the complaint around seven thousand times in the twenty years he'd been barbering at that stand. A farm boy whose roots reached to Livonia, in Washington County, he started cutting hair in Orleans when Clifford Dillinger had the shop. Dillinger spent a half century in the same narrow, deep room that originally housed the Bank of Orleans.

"A friend of mine, Freddie Brickie, had just finished barber school and opened a shop at Salem, and

I thought I'd like to be a barber, too," Elmo once said of his choice of trades. "I think it was a good decision. I like doing what I'm doing, and I've never been sorry. It doesn't seem that long; seems like it ought to be only four or five years. Cliff Dillinger is still around. He comes in regularly for his haircuts."

He looked around at the circle of faces, and he added, "I inherited most of these guys from him." He shook his head, which was far from bald. "Sometimes it gets pretty hectic around here. But it's a lot of fun. Before I came here, I worked in a shop in Louisville, Kentucky, and I'll guarantee you it was nothing like this. People there were not as friendly as the people here. This is pleasant. I know almost everyone by name, and there's always a practical joker around."

Though the old shop could accommodate three barbers, Elmo ruled as its sole haircutter. Working at the middle chair, he was usually flanked by waiting customers in the other two padded chairs. Others aligned themselves on theater seats (Elmo said they came out of a church) in the large room, either throwing the bull, reading the daily newspaper, or just sitting there listening. Given the regular run of baldies, Elmo figured he could turn out three to four haircuts an hour.

"Until I get one of these little guys (children) in the chair," he said. "Some will fight like a tiger against getting their hair cut. The other day one little guy, whose mother was trying to hold him in the chair, kicked me and bit her finger. I finally had to give up on him. At a time like that you can't think about speed. You just hope that the shop isn't full of waiting customers."

When a story of any substance was told in Elmo's, some listener was likely to remark, "Ain't that the damn'est thing you ever heard?"

Such was the case when Charlie recounted an experience he had at a revival one night in Orangeville. While the visiting venerable Lawrence County minister Otto (Ott) Duncan was delivering his message to the assembled souls, the loud yelping and yapping of passing foxhounds came through the window.

His message interrupted by the ruckus, Mr. Duncan stopped mid-sentence and listened until the commotion subsided. Then, Charlie said Mr. Duncan looked out over the congregation and said, "You know, I'd give fifty dollars for that lead hound."

Sure enough there was a listener in Elmo's that day who observed, "Ain't that the damn'est thing you ever heard?"

Charlie one day gave me an insight to the deep love he held for Orleans. He and his wife, Ethel, had been away for a brief time, and while on their return drive, a strange but wonderful warm sensation came over him.

"I had such a good feeling about coming home," Charlie said. "It was as though I was going to Heaven."

A short time later Ethel died. Because of the love they had for him, Charlie's despondency over the loss of his wife touched the hearts of his barber shop cronies. They tried their utmost to cheer him up. When he announced somewhat sadly that he had reluctantly decided to spend the coming winter with his sister, Mrs. Clyde Capps, in Venice, Florida, Elmo didn't hesitate to gladden his departure.

"Don't worry, Charlie, you ain't going to miss us," Elmo promised. "We'll telephone you collect every Monday morning."

Elmo gave him little rest. One morning when Charlie was feeling sad about his past, he lamented, "I've never made much of a contribution to society. But I would at least like to leave a pleasant memory when I go."

"Don't worry, Charlie, you will," Elmo assured him. "We'll all be glad to see you go."

Talk took many turns at Elmo's and sometimes religious denominations were the topic, After hearing all he wanted at one such session, Charlie spoke up and said, "It doesn't matter what we are. When we get where we're going we'll all be united brethren."

He went on then to tell a story about a man who was the only person in church one Sunday. Seeing his single listener, the minister was dubious about delivering the text he had prepared for the entire congregation. But, deciding that devotion and loyalty should have their reward, he preached the entire forty-five minute lesson to the lone man. Then addressing his audience of one, the preacher asked, "What did you think of my sermon?"

"Well," the man said pulling thoughtfully at his chin, "I'm a farmer and I raise cows. If one cow shows up to eat hay, I feed her. But," he set his jaw firmly and leveled his gaze at the preacher, "I wouldn't give her the whole load."

A second tale concerned a town sinner, a drunk. Ministers and priests had tried time and again to coax the man into their churches, but to no avail. One day a bright young priest approached him and said, "Come to church next Sunday and bring your bottle of whiskey with you."

The drunk had never received such a warm, understanding invitation. He thanked the young priest and accepted. Sure enough, when Sunday came he was ensconced in a pew, nipping from his precious bottle. He did not object when the priest called him to the altar. And when the priest extended a hand for the bottle, the drunk handed it over without argument.

"I want to show you something," the young priest said. "Watch."

From a cruet, he poured water into a glass. From the drunk's bottle, he poured whiskey into another glass.

"Watch," he repeated.

The drunk watched while the young priest held up a wiggling worm and dropped it into the glass of water. The tiny creature dove and swam and splashed and seemed to be having a joyous time.

"Now watch," the young priest said.

He took another wiggling worm and dropped it into the glass containing the whiskey.

The ohhs and ahhs of the congregation filled the church as the little worm shriveled up and died.

The drunk was wide-eyed with astonishment.

"Have you learned anything from what you just saw?" the young priest asked him.

Obviously incredulous at what he'd just witnessed, the drunk nodded. "I sure did," he almost shouted.

"Then would you mind facing all these good people and telling them what you just learned."

The drunk turned and studied the expectant faces turned up to him, passed a shaking hand over his mouth, lifted his voice to a near shout and announced, "If you don't want to get eat up with worms, drink whiskey!"

When the Methodist Church invested in a new sound system it was said that it was installed for Charlie's sake, and the rest of the Hard of Hearing Gang. And that reminded Charlie of the fellow who kept interrupting the preacher one Sunday by shouting amens all over the place.

A couple of ushers finally confronted him and threatened to throw him out into the street if he didn't shut up. The fellow told them, "Hey, I've got so much Spirit in me I'm about to bust."

One of those ushers shook a long finger under the man's nose and retorted, "Yeah? Well, you didn't get it here. Shut up!"

Charlie liked to involve Orangeville in some of his stories. When he was growing up there it was populated by some fifty to seventy-five people. When he moved to Orleans there were probably twenty-five.

"It was a good place to grow up," he once told the gathering at Elmo's. "We were poor, but it was a good life. We had no way of getting the news, like today, except by picking up the telephone and listening on the party line. For entertainment, we sat around the general store and told jokes. We had a summer once that was so dry the Baptists kept their baptisms to sprinkling only, and the Methodists used only a damp cloth."

He told of a clergyman who went from door to door to determine the number of believers in town. Addressing one householder who responded to his knock, he asked, "Are you Christian?"

"Nope," the man replied. "Christian lives next door."

The minister raised a hand and said, "No, that's not what I mean. I mean do you read the Bible?"

"Don't know how to read," the man said.

"Well, then," the minister pushed on, "are you ready for the Judgment?"

"When is it?" the man asked.

"Tomorrow," the cleric suggested. "The next day."

"Well," the householder scratched his head thoughtfully, "in that case I'd better go in and tell the old woman. Knowing her, she'll probably want to go both days."

Charlie was a couple years past eighty when he denied being that old. "I've just been around that long," he said. After a pause he added, "I try not to let my age bother me."

Age was on his mind for he went on to remember his wife, who had spent some months in a nursing home before she passed on.

"Sometimes it worries me," he told me that day. "I wouldn't want to be confined like that. I like to get around – to Elmo's, and to Cecil Johnson's Shell Station – just to loaf with my friends."

It was in Elmo's where I'd usually see Charlie. We'd laugh together at the stories that we heard there. Such as the story one club member told about a big catfish. He said his wife caught a sixty-five pounder on an open safety pin.

He no sooner had shut his mouth than another fellow said he and his dog were walking along the river bank one day and "danged" if the little mutt didn't jump into the water "and run a *hundred pound* catfish up on the bank."

That made the first fellow angry because he insisted his story was true. Before he could say too much more, a third story teller said he was fishing one night and pulled in a mud-covered object.

"It was just loaded with mud," he said, "so I began scraping it off. When I got it cleaned off, I was able to see that it was a lantern, and it was still lit, the wick burning as bright as you please."

"That," shouted the man whose little dog had run the hundred pound catfish up on the river bank, "is a damn lie!"

"That's your opinion," the lantern catcher retorted. "But I'll tell you what. You knock about ninety pounds off that catfish, and I'll blow the lantern out."

"Ain't that the damn'est thing you ever heard," somebody remarked just before another fellow bragged that he'd caught a bluegill that measured six inches.

"Six inches," snorted a listener. "Six inches ain't no big bluegill."

"Oh, excuse me," said the first speaker. "I should have explained. I meant it was six inches between the eyes."

Some of the Hard of Hearing Gang had been meeting at Elmo's in the afternoon then walking a few doors north to Herle's Cafe for coffee. Old age and illness had been slowly but inexorably hacking away at its numbers. One afternoon while Wayne Freed and Gene Compton were gabbing in Elmo's, Wayne looked at his watch and observed, "Well, Gene, it looks like Charlie's probably not going to show up. We might as well go get our coffee."

The fellows already knew that Charlie wouldn't show up. In so many words, Wayne had expressed a deep sorrow that each of them shared. Charlie Ragsdale had left Orleans forever, hopefully, for Heaven. And like Wayne said, he probably wouldn't show up for coffee that day.

Later, at Elmo's, some of us, in our way, extended that brief requiem for Charlie. We remembered the man who used to make us smile, the man who sometimes made us laugh so hard our bellies shook, the man who was so good for us. Charlie was good for Charlie, too. His humor kept him bright and smiling and it belied his eighty-three years.

Unhappily, Charlie's last days were spent in a nursing home. Fortunately, for those who loved him at least, he was there only a matter of weeks. Had he a choice, he probably would have preferred his last breath to have been taken while standing at a first tee on a sunny golf course, announcing with a smile, as he always did to his golfing companions, "This is where friendship ceases – and hell begins."

Golf was really his nemesis. In Elmo's one morning he confided in mock despair, "I'm lucky to shoot under a hundred." Then loud enough so that the working Elmo could hear, he added, "I play the town barber a lot. I've only beat him twice. After that he got ugly and made me give him a stroke."

He smiled and winked at me. "He's so ugly, when he was born the doctor slapped his mother," he said.

No matter how many years a story had been around, when Charlie repeated it, it was funny. Like the perennial about the devoted golfer who took time from his game to remove his hat and bow his head in deference to a passing funeral procession.

"Someone you know?" his partner asked. "Tomorrow," the man replied as he resumed his game, "we'd have been married thirty-five years."

Charlie's sense of humor followed him almost to the grave. During the eulogy at his funeral in Bethel Church near Orangeville, the preacher gave mourners a sampling of it.

"Charlie was a teller of tales," the minister who knew Charlie said of him. "Trouble was," he went on, "we can't tell some of them here."

There was one he could have told. A preacher friend was invited to play golf with Charlie and some of the gang one day. He said he'd never played before, but when scores were tallied after the last hole was played, he had beaten Charlie. Frowning skeptically, a chagrined Charlie declared, "If I didn't know you were a truthful man, I'd say you're a liar."

Most of Charlie's tales were tellable anyplace. Many were unashamedly churchy. Elmo, who helped carry his good friend to his grave, remembered one Charlie told about a parishioner who had fallen asleep during the sermon.

"Wake him up," the preacher called to an usher.

"You wake him up," the usher countered. "You put him to sleep."

Someone once said that story-telling was Charlie's claim to fame. It was but one. Before his retirement to Orleans, he was also a successful Orangeville farmer. He was a loving husband and father, too. He also was a good brother to six siblings. And, having been blessed with a good voice and heart, he made the time to sing at almost seven hundred weddings and funerals. His credits go on.

It was Phil Bruner, one of Charlie's golfing buddies, who in a few words, revealed the true measure of Charlie's inspiring influence.

"We're all better off for having known him," he said.

Charlie once said of Elmo's barber shop, "It's a good place to spend time. I have a lot of friends who go there, Democrats and Republicans. There's a lot of difference between them, you know. Democrats are pretty good people. I think we're all good friends, though."

Pictured, left to right, Charlie Ragsdale, Wayne Freed and John Elrod in Elmo Wolfe's Barber Shop. (March, 1984)

THE BUS DRIVER

Catherine had known Mac all her life. They were born within a half mile of each other on Kelly Bend in Greene County. When he began driving a school bus in 1937, Catherine was a student at Worthington High School. When Mac bought a new six-cylinder, fifty-four passenger, one thousand five hundred dollar bus, Catherine was among the first to ride in it. School buses then were equipped with bench seats along the outer walls and a single row of seats down the middle.

Until the new bus began making its rounds of Kelly Bend, Catherine walked more than a mile to Farmer's Ferry where she boated across the West Fork of White River to reach a bus on the other side. It was an exciting day for her when she could dispense with that and catch her ride at Kelly Bend.

Two years later the bus played a role in another exciting day for Catherine. She and Mac eloped in it to Crawfordsville where they obtained a marriage license from the Montgomery County clerk. From there Mac drove to Greencastle in Putnam County where they found a preacher who married them. Then they rushed back to Greene County in time for Mac to haul boys and girls home from school that afternoon. Mac was thirty-eight, a widower with a son and daughter. Catherine was seventeen and freshly graduated from high school.

Nine days before they recounted these events to me in late July of 1975, Catherine rode Mac's bus again. It was an event that gave rise to mixed emotions. Harold "Mac" McIntosh Sr., then nearing his seventy-second birthday, was ending thirty-eight consecutive years as a school bus driver. Children who were usually bright and cheery as they boarded his bus for the morning ride to school were, on the morning of Friday, May 23, 1975, quiet, sober, thoughtful. Their behavior was hardly that of sixty-four youngsters on their way to the last day of school before the start of summer vacation.

Their Mac – the same Mac who had hauled their fathers and mothers to school – was leaving, retiring. The same Mac who had been friend, advisor, father confessor, even father and mother to some of them, would no longer guide them toward classes, toward a meaningful future. They hugged and kissed him, and they wept. Catherine wept. Mac wept.

"Why, Mac?" they wanted to know. "Why?"

Later that morning, before Mac drove the long yellow school bus away from Bloomfield High School for the last time, his riders presented him with a bronze plaque handsomely mounted on mahogany.

"To Mac," it read. "In grateful appreciation of our experience during our last years of your thirty-eight. For the smile, the friendship, the advice, the fun, the gratuities..."

"I always greeted them when they got on the bus of a morning," Mac began recalling the many hauling days as a school bus driver. "And I did the same in the evening when I took them home. I tried to be logical with every question they came up with, and I answered every question."

Driver-student relationships went much deeper than that. Many of the youngsters discussed with him personal problems they would never have discussed with their parents. He personally had dealt with six pregnancies, and became liaison and peacemaker between the affected youngsters and outraged parents. He had the gift of knowing just by looking when a boy or girl was having trouble at home. When he questioned delicately and confirmed his fears he would begin the healing process by saying, "Give it another try, maybe tomorrow things will be better."

Boys and girls who had made up their minds to run away from home took his advice. They not only gave it another try, they were still living happily in their native Greene County. Once, when food was being regularly stolen from the school cafeteria, Mac became aware of the emaciated appearance of one of his riders. Without ceremony he began providing the youngster with daily lunch money. The thefts stopped. A boy who was treasurer of the senior class came up eighty dollars short when payment of class photos fell due. Fearful of all but Mac, he finally went to the bus driver and confided his error. Mac lent him the money. Some months later the boy repaid his benefactor and went on to a successful future. Through the years Mac had lent money for several reasons — as much as one hundred dollars — and every penny was repaid.

"Their parents would snap them off and they would come to me," Mac recalled, his blue eyes and ruddy face reflecting remembered sympathies. "When they have confidence in you, they want you to have confidence in them," he revealed his simple philosophy of dealing with youngsters.

His tone softened as he began relating a memory of a girl who had but two blouses and one skirt in her wardrobe. She wished to complete school but was battling parents who preferred she go out and get a job. Mac and Catherine took her under their wing.

They tried to help her in every way, but in the end her parents won out, she quit school and went to work. Years later, as Mac was loading his kids at school for the trip home he learned that she was killed instantly when a train struck her car at a grade crossing. Two of the youngsters he was loading were her sons. Again Mac became the surrogate parent, caring, explaining, helping and shedding his own personal tears.

The problem children of other school bus drivers were a challenge to Mac, and he didn't fail them. "I never had to call one down, and I never had to threaten one. I'd just go to looking when one got out of line and the older kids would see and they'd take care of the problem," he explained his success.

The profundity of his concern for young people is best revealed in an incident that happened not on a school bus but during a squirrel hunting expedition.

"I was settin' and watchin' for squirrels," Mac began the recollection in typical Hoosier fashion, when a youth, thinking Mac's red cap was a squirrel, shot Mac. He remembered the young man running toward him in panic, hysterically begging forgiveness, all the while informing Mac that his father had taught him how to hunt right, and that he couldn't understand how he could go and do a terrible thing like shoot a man, and ending the long outburst by saying, "I'm just going to shoot myself."

Bleeding from the throat, right arm and chest, Mac replied, "Hellfire, don't do that. You've already shot one man today."

Mac's buses carried children to Ft. Wilson School, Smith School, Calvertville School, and Worthington and Bloomfield schools. The bonds that were forged between him and his riders over four hundred and eighty-two thousand miles and thirty-eight years, and the experiences they shared, were incredible.

"It's hard to sum up twelve years in one letter," one of Mac's girl riders wrote him. "Some kids don't understand how a bus driver could mean so much to a person. But I know that unless they ride Bus 2, they don't have any idea how special a bus driver can be. I think back for twelve years and I can't think of a time when I got on the bus there wasn't a smile and a few words. You may not realize just how important that was to me. The times I have left the house upset or depressed there was always a smile waiting to make me feel better. My most valuable and best memories of you as a bus driver came this past year. But for some reason I knew you understood. I could just tell. I was at the place where I just didn't care what happened to me . . . knowing that you cared helped a lot . . . thanks for all the caring. I know it's hard to give up a job you love so much. It's just as hard on us kids. But remember how much love you have put into so many kids."

It was hard for Mac to give up hauling kids to and from school. "My last day," he said of May 23, 1975, "was my saddest and most pleasant day in all the years I've been driving a school bus."

Tears welled in his eyes. Catherine, seated opposite me on a couch in the remodeled McIntosh log house dabbed at her eyes. There had to be more to Mac's quitting, and this is what happened. The previous December when school bus route bids were due, Mac submitted his. Although it had been low enough to assure him of another four years as a contract driver, and he had passed his public chauffeur's license exam and three physicians who examined him said he was fit to drive a bus, Mac was turned down. The school board had arbitrarily set an age limit for bus drivers and Mac was out, against his will.

There were no officials present in the school yard that day to mark the end of Mac's thirty-eight years, just the kids with the plaque, with letters and words of farewell. Then Mac drove them all to Worthington for a final treat. On the last ride home his passengers wept openly. As the big yellow bus pulled away from their homes, the kids' mothers stood at the roadside dabbing at their eyes and waving farewell. Mac at the wheel and Catherine seated behind him also wept.

It had been a long ride, one during which Mac hauled his own wife as a high school student, his own children, his grandchildren, and, making him more unique among school bus drivers, a great grandchild.

Looking back over the route of Bus 2 from where he sat in the living room of his home, Mac said longingly, "Every foot of the road, every building, had a meaning. I'd see people and their lives would flash in front of me like a movie."

LOTTIE ROBERTS

She's no longer here, so she can't call on the phone or write, like she used to, and say, "If you're blue, just come over and have a piece of pumpkin pie and a cup of tea."

But I still think of her once in a while, most recently when a visiting daughter of mine baked a pumpkin pie and as I was savoring it, there, suddenly, was Lottie Roberts, standing in front of me as big as life, in my memory.

I smiled inwardly at the sudden recollection of another day when she stood before me – in real life. It was a day long ago, which was not blue, but which I now believe was made especially for a visit with her. Between the time of my phone call to announce my intention and the time I arrived at her front door at Eighth and Harold streets, in Bloomington, she had managed to stick a pumpkin pie in the oven and set out tea cups and sugar loaves.

"Well," I recall her saying as she surveyed me standing on her doorstep, "you've finally come to see old Mrs. Roberts, eh?"

"Yes," I said. "Finally." And as she ushered me inside, I could almost taste the delicious aroma emanating from her oven. "I've come," I added, "to see who's been calling me and writing me all those letters."

She had written me two. I was sometimes attracted to people that way, and some of my visits with them ended up as columns. While we waited for her pie to bake and the kettle to whistle, we visited and I was given a thumb-nail sketch of Lottie's life.

She was reared on a potato and stock farm in a place called Bullock's Corners, in Ontario, Canada. It was there, as a young woman, that she began, with her husband, a career in the mission field. After devoting thirty-five years to that pursuit, she arrived in Bloomington, some seventeen years before our meeting.

"We had snow from October until May," she said of her early days in Bullock's Corners. "We couldn't go to school after November because of it. We'd spend our time close to the wood stove, studying, then we'd try to get back to school a couple of weeks before Easter, to take spring exams."

When the first cold snap struck, her father would butcher five pigs and a beef to sustain his family of six children for the winter. In plenty of time for that season, her mother would make winter underwear from their father's cast-off longjohns for her four brothers, Lottie said.

"We all wore homemade underwear back then, and they'd come right down almost to our ankles," she laughed at the memory of what she and her sister wore. "Red Path Sugar and Star Brand Flour came in hundred-pound cloth sacks then, and Mother would make our undies from them. Say," she naughtily slitted one eye at me, "I was raised with Star Brand Flour written across my hiney until I was eighteen years old." Then, attempting to rescue whatever dignity was left from that intimate revelation, she smiled sweetly and said, "We crocheted a lot then, too, and we had pretty lace on those flour-sack undies."

Lottie seemed to have great fun telling me that her father was an Orangeman, but that "Old Gran'maw McConnell was a Catholic. She had the farm right next to ours," she remembered, "and we loved her. Each time sickness struck one of John M. Bullock's children, dear Old Gran'maw McConnell would come over and baptize us. All of us were baptized Catholic by her."

She and Rev. William A. Roberts shared the years in the mission field as servants of the Congregation Church, now known as the United Church of Christ. Together they founded the first Easter Pageant in Lawton, Oklahoma, later known as the Annual Wichita Mountains Easter Sunrise Service. "The first one," she said of the original service, "was held in the snow and cold, and I'll never forget that one."

Mission work took the couple to Louisiana, Texas and Oklahoma, where they spent ten years in the infamous dust bowl of the Great Depression era. As a young woman, Lottie toyed with writing and tried to get her works published. She wrote one piece about Bullock's Corners that caught the eye of the editors of *Liberty Magazine* (defunct these many years), and in part it went like this:

"I remember families baking on the death of a member, making preparations for the 'wake', which usually lasted two days and two nights. On one occasion, the dead man was propped up in a corner, (his) pipe placed in his mouth, and his favorite winter cap, one with fur lugs, placed at the correct angle on his head, while his friends and neighbors feasted, drank, danced and played cards. The widow got very hilarious and drunk..."

When Lottie had concluded reciting from memory that paragraph, she again impishly slitted the same naughty eye in my direction and said, "I'm wicked. I make a joke out of everything. I guess I was born laughing."

Maybe she was and maybe she wasn't. I do know that she was good for a laugh for me that day, not to mention a piece of homemade pumpkin pie and a cup of hot tea. When the blue day she'd always invited me to spend with her finally did overtake me, Lottie was gone. But with the help of this memory of her, I was able to work my way through it.

GOLDEN WEDDING

As they drove toward Bedford from their respective homes in Indian Springs and Kale in Martin County, Keith Piper and Della May Hamilton were visibly nervous.

The 1929 Durant sedan was comfortable enough, so it wasn't the car that made them that way. And it was a beautiful, sunlit Monday morning, so it wasn't the weather.

But no two ways about it. Keith, dressed in a blue suit he'd purchased six months earlier for his graduation from Shoals High School, and Della May, attired in a borrowed black felt hat and burnt-orange dress with white lace collar and turned back white lace cuffs, were n-e-r-v-o-u-s.

Only the previous night they'd traveled this same route in a topless Model-T Ford touring car, with Velma Dillon and Cleo Bateman in the back seat, to see Rudy Vallee in "The Vagabond Lover" at a Bedford theater.

That was when Keith had shouted to Della over the clatter and the jouncing of the Ford, and the rush of breeze past their ears, "Let's get married tomorrow."

"I don't even have a hat," Della May shouted back at him as she moved closer to Keith. But she agreed they should be married on the next day.

"The courthouse in Bedford was being built about then," Keith remembered as he told me this story in his one-chair barber shop in Avoca. "We couldn't find the clerk's office to get a license. We were pretty nervous. So we drove to Paoli, in Orange County, and got cold feet there. So we started for home. We decided then to go to Shoals and get a license there."

It was a circuitous route they'd followed that 24th day of February, 1930, to obtain a marriage license in their own home county. Then with a Rev. Howard conducting the ceremony – his first – and his wife and Neva Dillon standing as witnesses, Keith and Della May, despite everyone being nervous, were married.

"I don't know who was most nervous, me or the preacher," Keith, a white-haired, blue-eyed man remembered.

Della May's mother wept when she arrived home and said, "We're married, Mom."

Luckily Mrs. Hamilton liked Keith. He'd been walking a mile in all kinds of weather from his home in Indian Springs to the Hamilton home in Kale to see her daughter for two years. So she figured his intentions had to be honorable. It was all right that Della May had married him.

"Mom always thought he was just a fine boy," Della May recalled.

Keith then went to break the news to his father, a barber in Indian Springs who had taught that trade to four of his five sons, one of whom was Keith.

"I kinda suspected that was agoin' on," Curt Piper told his son.

The elder Piper had also thought it strange that Keith would come to him on a Monday morning and ask to use the family Durant.

On June 24 of that year, Keith and his bride arrived in Avoca where he set up shop as a barber, and that's where he stayed. Keith's one-chair shop, which he jokingly called his "jail-house," was attached to an inviting, sprawling gray frame home almost dead-center in that rural Lawrence County community.

After almost a half-century of barbering there, and his early years in Indian Springs, Keith's customers came from near and far. When we talked, a few of them were in the shop: Sharon Staley and her sons, Brian, then four, and Curtis five, of Avoca, and Rev. Matt Strunk, of Peerless.

He had adjusted to the changes in men's hair styles without taking lessons, and he was happy that he had but one lady customer. "They used to get their hair cut in the barber shop years ago," Keith said, "but I'm glad they don't anymore."

"They used to get bobs," Della May laughed. "Shingle-bob, bootsie-bob and windblown bob. The bootsie-bob was like a man's haircut but with two spit curls in front of the ears. They didn't have hair spray then." So they used spit.

Della May remembered those first days in Avoca.

"We batched in one room and lived in another. We didn't even have a table to eat off of. But we had the happiest times. They were good days. We had lots of friends and we made fudge and popcorn and pulled toffee, and we played Rook all night," she said through a smile and misty eyes.

"Once in awhile we sit and get to talking about the way we got married and the way we started out and we get to laughing," she continued. "The kids, when we tell them about it, always think it's the funniest thing they ever heard. They all had nice church weddings."

They had three children: Don Piper, Ronald Piper, and Mrs. Judy Curry.

Keith and Della May were not wealthy. But Keith contended that barbering had been good to them.

"We've lived comfortably," he said, and recounted that it took and still took daily hours from 7:30 a.m.

through 8 p.m. to attain that comfort. "There's nothing more depressing than sitting here waiting for a customer," he said.

For a man who walked a mile between his home in Indian Springs and Della May's in Kale for so many nights in all kinds of weather, just sitting still, even after many years of working, was more than he could bear.

But Della May thought he worked too hard, anyway, and she complained she'd never cooked him a meal she didn't have to re-heat because of customer interruptions.

Keith's ambition was to someday retire, but the prospects, considering his earnings, were slim. He charged only a dollar and fifty cents for a haircut. So, he figured to keep working.

Della May had two wishes: one, which she knew was impossible – that she had saved her burnt-orange wedding dress, and two – that they could live to celebrate their golden wedding anniversary.

Remembering all they had told me, including an account of Keith's drive from Tunnelton one night in rain and sleet in the topless Model-T Ford touring car to see his sweetie, I had the feeling Keith and Della May had been enjoying a golden wedding ever since that nervous Monday in February of 1930.

ONLY ONE

People around Bloomfield used to say, "There's only one man like him in this world." People in other places said that, too, if and when they met Clovis "Buck" Frye. And they were probably right. I know for certain that I knew of only one.

Few of those people knew, though, that except for the bad aim of a shotgun-wielding assailant back when he was fourteen, there might not have been even one Buck Frye. I didn't know. Not until Buck related the incident to me in the shade of a huge tree that grew in the side yard of his home on West Turner Street.

"Charlie Beck had called and asked if I wanted to go to a chivaree that night," Buck began an account of that near fatal incident. "Of course I did. A chivaree was always a lot of fun. Always music: a fiddle, guitar and banjo. And they'd shoot shotguns straight up in the air and the shot would come down and splatter on tin roofs," Buck spoke in rapid-fire recollection.

For a man of eighty-seven there was an almost breathless rush to his narration that almost defied note-taking. Like the tale about his horse, Toni. But, then, Toni was a winning race horse, and I suppose it was only fitting that Buck should tell that story at a gallop.

He'd bought Toni from Ben Hayes in Worthington "The year of the big flood," 1913, long before some of us were even born.

CLOVIS "BUCK" FRYE

"And I raced her over there," Buck related. "And that horse won. A nice amount of money, too. And after the race, I put her in the hitching barn, they had one over there then. When I went to get her later, someone had cut her harness to pieces. There wasn't a single piece left that was over a foot long."

Their relationship was to be shortlived. While Buck was sparking Inez Hunter over near Mineral City one night, a mysterious tragedy struck the speedy animal.

"Sometime in the forepart of the night, when I got ready to go home, the horse and buggy were gone," Buck remembered. "So I walked five miles to where I lived."

The next day he was summoned to Plummer Creek near Mineral City, and there he saw his horse, Toni, drowned in twelve inches of water.

Buck was uncertain about how the animal got loose from where he had hitched it, or how or why it got into the creek.

"I thought a lot of that horse," he said in eulogy to the memory of Toni.

A horse and buggy were important to a fellow back then, if a fellow expected to get around. And Buck got around. Only that's not exactly how he said it.

"I had a lot of territory in those days," is the way he said it. "And I had a lot of business."

That lasted only until he met a girl named Nona who lived near Antioch in Taylor Township.

"She's a wonderful wife," Buck indicated what came of that meeting. "And we have four wonderful children."

He identified them: Gerald, the oldest; Dale "Tex," the youngest; and two daughters in between, Mrs. Reese (Gloria) Hall and Mrs. Jordan (Joyce) Emery.

Buck himself was one of eight children: Goldie, Paris, Clovis, Elva, Zelma, Jewie, Faye and Roy in the order in which he gave me their names. Clovis, of course, being Buck.

It was Buck's youngest son who informed him at lunch one day several years ago that the covered bridge south of town had collapsed and fallen into White River (See "Click Click" Page 81).

"You don't know any more good jokes, do you?" Buck responded. "I just crossed that bridge on the way home."

"Let's just go down and see," Tex urged.

"I've driven a dump truck ever since I was twenty, and I had delivered five tons of gravel across the river that day," Buck recalled. "That was the load limit on the bridge. When I came back I was running empty, and that bridge must have fallen just after I crossed it. I didn't even know it. When Tex and I got there, it was down in the river. I looked down at it and thought, 'There's where I could've been.'"

Buck had some other narrow escapes in his time. None of them took place very far from home and one of them was right in his own backyard; a riding mower very nearly plunged him over a thirty-foot embankment there.

A retiree for at least the last twenty years at this time, Buck had a number of hobbies that kept him busy. One, which had been a life-long hobby, was cattle; by this time only a few cows and a bull. He had one cow twenty-two years, nineteen of which she produced a calf, the latest on the Fourth of July.

"She's an old family cow," Buck spoke affectionately of the bovine. "And I'm keeping her for the good that she's done. She's been faithful to me."

Buck attributed all the good in his life "to God and His Son," and his personal success, "to my personality."

He explained the latter: "I could go to Kalamazoo, Michigan, sit down in a restaurant and I'd soon know the fellow sitting next to me. I have a lot of gab, and that's what it's for, to be used right."

And because of his personality and his honesty, "Everything good," Buck added, "has happened to me. Everything has turned out my way. If not today, it turned out right tomorrow."

It almost didn't. The night he and Charlie Beck took part in the boisterous chivaree was very nearly Buck's last night of his life. Charlie, too. They were falsely accused of throwing something at a horse and were shot by its owner who accosted them on the way home.

"I had thirty-nine holes in me, thirty-nine number six shot," Buck remembered. "Charlie had thirteen in him. He was lucky. The man shot from my side of the road. I still have some in me. Feel."

Buck guided my finger to a corner of his left eye, to his head and his neck to feel the large, round shot under the skin.

"I lost my voice for eight-ten months," he said of the throat wound. "But we had a trial and that fellow went to prison for a long time.

"That was a lot of shot to take, but I'm a tough old devil," he smiled.

MARIGOLD

When the day came to "write" for her diploma her father was working the buggy horse in the wheat and she had no way to make the journey to Marco.

"It just broke my heart," Marigold Beck Page spoke across the table in the kitchen of her home in Bloomington. "I could have passed it, I'm certain of that. And it would have been grand."

Her ambition was to teach. Because she could not make the trip from Pleasantville to Marco to join dozens of other eighth graders who took the final exam, which was known as "writing for graduation," her future was altered.

"I have no regrets," she said looking back on her past. "I had a good life at home, and I later married a good man. But," her blue eyes lit up as she expressed a familiar lament, "if I had known then what I know now, I would have fought for that buggy horse – for an education."

At thirteen she became a farm hand, helping her father. At fifteen she began working as a domestic in other people's homes in the Pleasantville neighborhood. Later, her mother decided that she and her three sisters should learn to sew. And a new Singer treadle sewing machine was purchased and brought into the farm home.

"That was my job after we came here to Bloomington," Mrs. Page said. "I was a seamstress."

She recalled that in the beginning, in 1937, she had some business cards printed and distributed them on the Indiana University Campus.

"It wasn't long until I had more sewing than I could do," she said.

For the next twenty years she made frocks, gowns, suits, coats, shirts and wedding dresses.

"I loved to make lovely dresses," she remembered fondly. "They were so beautiful, trimmed up with lace and tucks."

She was nearing sixty when she quit sewing, more than twenty years before we met. Since then she had spent what time she wasn't hospitalized or in a convalescent home, in her kitchen.

"I live in the kitchen," she had said at the outset of our visit. "It's a wonderful place to live."

It was in her kitchen that she read and wrote letters to friends and relatives.

"I love them," she said of the letters that arrived in response to those she wrote. "I look every day for a letter from somebody I've written to. And I read them over and over and over and over. Then I put them away and get them out some other day and read them over again. They bring me a lot of happiness and pleasure. They make me feel all good inside."

She smiled and seemed to squirm pleasantly in her seat as she spoke. Some letters came from a distance, from a niece, Mrs. Gene (Lela) Allen, a former Linton resident, then a teacher in Paoli, PA. Some came from a good friend in New Mexico, former Bloomington resident Nell Tourilev.

Because of a past surgery to her right hand, letter writing was somewhat slow and difficult for her. Still she managed to produce a half dozen a week. There had been other surgeries in her eighty-two years. There were also some falls that ended in broken bones; one in a separated shoulder. She remembered the last.

"I was in the hospital for three weeks," she shook her head slightly. "Then I was taken to the Bloomington Convalescent Center, and I was there for six weeks. They were just wonderful at the hospital," she gave a satisfied sigh. "And when I went to the center, they treated me like a baby. They were so kind. There was never a cross word. They were just precious. I cried like a baby when I had to leave." She said she got so "lonely and lonesome" after she was brought home that, "I cried some more, I missed them all so much. They were just something special."

From her kitchen table she could look out a window on a row of white peonies at the rear of her yard.

"There are some red ones around the other side of the house," she said informatively. Then with another sigh she added, "But I haven't seen them growing there this year because I can't get out there."

"Peonies," she continued, "are my favorite flowers. I don't know why I was named Marigold." She made a face. "It is one of the stinkin'est flowers that ever bloomed," she said. "Besides that, I was born in January."

Another thought occurred to her and she laughed. "I used to go by the name Mary, I disliked my name so. Then as I got older I thought, what the heck. Marigold's all the name I have. Why not use it."

Her apparent satisfaction with her lot and her happy mood aroused my curiosity. She said her light mood had been a constant in her life.

"I think it's nice to be happy and pleasant," she smiled. "It makes other people happy."

She attributed her ability to stay that way, at least in part, to her daughter, Lela Ruth Brosman, who lived next door.

"She comes in every morning, combs my hair and cooks. She does my washing. She cut a bouquet of those red peonies and brought them in so that I could see them. I think I might get pretty low without her," she said.

Mrs. Page and her sisters were born and reared on a farm in Stafford Township in Greene County. She attended the old Ohio School, at that time a one room frame building of eight grades and thirty-two other kids. Ohio School was a quarter mile from her home and she walked that distance daily. Graduation writings, however, traditionally were offered at Marco, several miles distant, a trip she was not allowed to make on foot.

"I remember the day when they gave the writings," she said whimsically. "It was late March. I remember because it was always late March when we took off our long underwear. My father needed the horse. The farm came first. And he didn't think it was necessary that we should have an education. He was kind and nice, but he felt a woman's place was in the home."

The last time she had seen that home, it was falling in on itself and in the process of being removed from where it was built by her father. Recalling that sight, she was reminded of another.

"We had a winter snow there when I was eleven or twelve that was higher than the fence rails. A rain came afterward and it froze solid. And we walked to school on ice across the fence rails," she said. "We had horrible winters, and they always stayed until March."

A friend, Cora Brewer Lent, also of Bloomington, also walked those icy ways to school with her. "We talk a lot on the phone," Mrs. Page said of their enduring friendship. "We can talk about the same subjects and they sound so good."

She assured me that she didn't feel eighty-two, that, "Somehow I just feel contented and satisfied." She offered some advice for the aging.

"If you stay young inside, you will never grow old," she said. "You'll get tired and weaker, but," she smiled, "you'll never grow old."

THE AUCTION SIGN

John Abner pinched some small pieces from a large light-brown leaf and carefully tucked them inside his jaw. Similar leaves, golden in the early morning sunlight stuck out from a side pocket of his jacket.

"Yeah," he said genially, speaking between pinches and tucks, "it's long green . . . home grown tobacco . . . it's all I ever use . . . it's the best. Want some?"

"Me, chew tobacco?"

Horrors!

I told him of my experience with chewing tobacco.

I dreamed one night of chewing the stuff. I don't know till this day what precipitated such a dream. I had been around tobacco chewers many times but I had never had a yen to chew the stuff. It looked so distasteful. So . . . so . . . Yuk.

But I had this dream of chewing tobacco. Had a jaw full of it. Puffed way out. Like some baseball players on television. Only I wasn't playing baseball. And I wasn't on television. I was hanging wallpaper – on a ceiling.

In my dream I was standing on a walkingboard that was stretched between two stepladders. To better see what I was doing I had arched my back to such a degree that my face was turned up so that it was parallel to the ceiling.

I was having some difficulty keeping the paper up on the ceiling. Oh, was I ever having trouble. While

I struggled with that task, my mouth filled dangerously with the brown juice.

Before I could take any precaution against doing so, I suddenly swallowed. Gulp!

I raised up out of my sleep, hocking and gagging like a cat with a fur ball caught in its throat. I shivered and I shook and I sweated and for at least five minutes I was afraid I would not throw up. Woke up the whole house with my carryings on, too.

I never chewed tobacco again. Not in real life. Not in my dreams.

I never papered any more ceilings, either.

Suppressing a shiver that rose in me with the telling of that dream, I raised a palm toward John Abner and said no thanks to his offer. And I looked away from his puffed-out jaw and switched the talk to the auction sale sign I'd seen on my arrival in Leesville.

I'd been talking with Phil Concannon when I saw the thing. A line foreman with Public Service Indiana, Phil was supervising the construction of an overhead three-phase electrical transmission line from Leesville to Medora.

The job had been in progress for six months and was expected to be finished in another four. After its completion, PSI expected to push some sixty-nine thousand volts the fifteen miles over which the line ran.

I hadn't seen Phil for years but I had no problem recognizing him. He probably hadn't gained or lost a pound in the twenty-five years he'd been with PSI. He still wore his hair in a burr cut and his eyes were still as Irish-blue as Paddy's dear ol' "mither's." He and linemen Alan Chase and Virgil Baker had stopped their big yellow PSI truck in Leesville when I happened along.

There on the fringe of the popular rolling hills of southern Indiana that I like so well, we held a kind of brief reunion. And it was while we were thus involved that I saw the auction sign. It was a surprise. Those things always are to me. I suppose it is my inherent opposition to change. I like the status quo. I like to think that things will always remain the same, that they should not change.

At twelve o'clock noon on Saturday, August 21, 1982, change was certainly headed for Leesville, according to the sign. John Abner and his wife, Vena, planned to sell their general store at what the sign described as a business auction.

"We like to go to Florida in the winter," John Abner gave their reason for selling out. Another reason he gave – after he was no longer suspicious of me and understood that I wasn't trying to sell him a newspaper advertisement – is that he simply didn't have the time to operate the store. The store had been in Leesville over a century. Among its previous owners were Orville Cain and Wayne Armstrong.

"It's fully modern now, and having it that way is like being at home and making your living," John Abner told me rather cryptically. Then he went on to add, "There's absolutely nothing to keep anybody from making a living in a store in the country."

The first settlement in Lawrence County, Leesville was certainly country. Still, the small rural community at one time had supported two stores, and once, during a pool tournament held in a recreation building owned by John Abner and also on the auction block, thirty-two sharks competed at three tables. Recreational facilities there also included about a dozen electronic game machines, a juke box, a cigarette machine, a long church pew, and sandwiches.

John Abner's business card gave his name as W. S. "John" Abner, and I should have asked him about the

W. S. and the "John," but I think I got sidetracked when he led me out behind the building to show me his flourishing vegetable garden.

It was a fairly good-sized plot, full of many good things to eat. I secretly surveyed the rows looking for tobacco growths, but I probably wouldn't have recognized them. And I really wasn't that interested. I wasn't going to ask to take some home to chew.

While this was the first time I had visited with John, it was not the first time I had been to Leesville. It must have been a couple of years since my last visit there, maybe longer. I could not remember. Nor could I remember what I had written about the small community on that previous visit.

However, I do remember that I arrived there without a dime in cash in my pockets and an empty gas tank. Being without ready cash was not unusual for newspaper reporters. None of us made much money. Vena Abner didn't know me from Adam. But I dared approach her in the store. I explained my situation and in desperation I asked if she would take my check for a tank of gasoline.

Unsmiling, Vena studied me with no little amount of suspicion, saw she didn't know me, and she asked coldly, "Where are you from?"

"Bloomington," I replied honestly.

Vena said but a single word.

"No."

And, without another look in my direction, she turned her attention to other matters.

From that day on I have been pretty careful about telling people where I am from.

EASTER GIRL

After Betty Kay Fox was stricken with infantile paralysis at age eight doctors said she would not see her twelfth birthday. When she outlived that dire prediction, they gave her another four years to live. At sixteen Betty gave no indication of dying. Rather than set another date for that event, doctors shrugged and chose only to expect her demise at some later time. Surprisingly, she lived to be forty. Not because Betty made an effort to live that long. On the contrary.

"She had always wanted to die," her mother, Helen Fox, said after Betty's remains were interred in Valhalla Memory Gardens, in Bloomington.

"When she heard or read of other persons dying she'd say, 'Why, Mother? Why them and not me? They had something to live for. I don't have anything to live for.' Betty had wanted to die ever since she first got sick with polio."

Betty's long illness began on a Thursday many years ago. At that time it was called infantile paralysis and began with what she described as "a splitting headache." Arriving home from school in pain one day she summoned her dog – a hound named Joe – and they took a stroll together. It was the last time she would ever walk.

She lay in bed for more than three decades, totally dependent upon her mother and her father, Forrest,

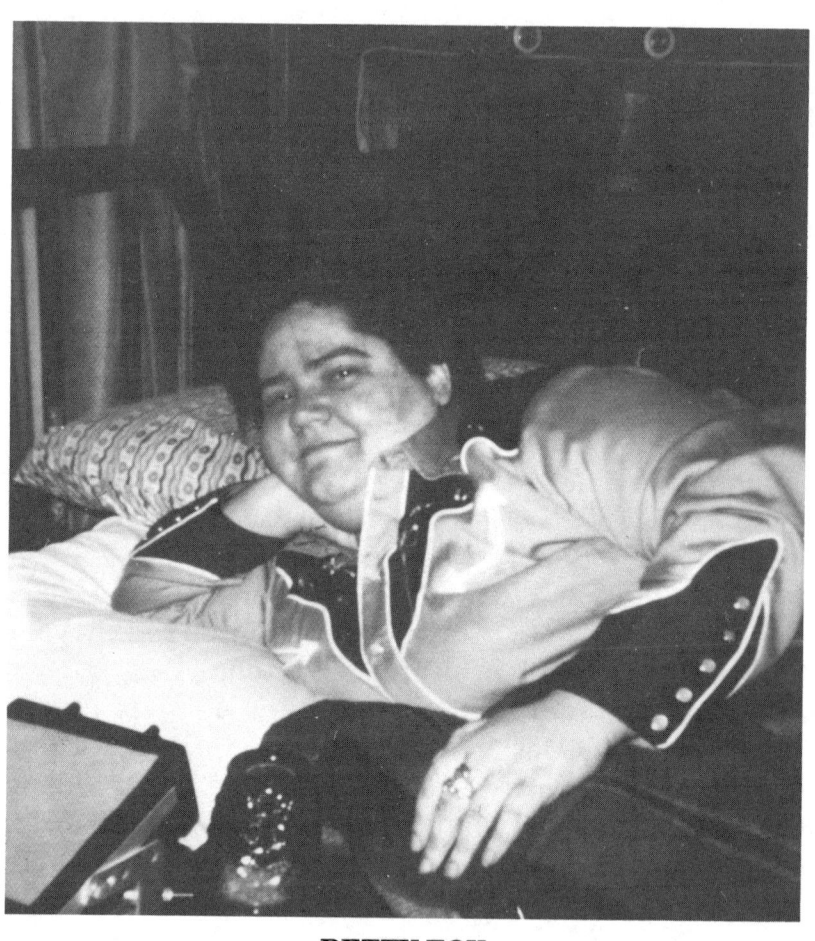

BETTY FOX
In Her World.

in whose rural Bloomington home she lived. On the last morning that she went to minister to her, as she had each morning of Betty's bedfast life, Helen Fox found her daughter dead.

"She seemed asleep," she said. "There was a touch of a smile on her lips. But she was dead." The mother recalled the events of Betty's last days. "She was not well the past week. She was not herself. But she would never let me call the doctor. 'Medicine,' she would say, 'is poison. It keeps you on the earth just that much longer.' She refused to take anything. She wanted to die."

In those many years between the Thursday she was stricken and the Sunday that she died, Betty lay almost completely removed from the world. Polio had left her an adult from the waist up and a child of eight from the waist down, and paralyzed. Thirty-two years of twenty-four hour days in bed, ten of those years in hospitals, had been tediously long and painfully lonely.

To fill the empty hours she directed her attention toward collections of various kinds, viewing colorful slides, listening to records, watching television, reading, and writing to pen pals. But none of these brightened her life as did the discovery one day of police calls on an old black, box-like radio equipped with a short wave band. Those voices had raised the curtain on a new world for her.

Although she had never met any of them personally, she was able by listening to the radio to learn the names of Monroe County sheriff's deputies and their car numbers. She learned much of the International Ten Code used by police agencies, and a considerable amount of the localized Signal System Designation, simply by listening to the six-band.

During my first visit with her, a police call crackled and she interrupted our talk to listen. "That's Unit

9," she said for my benefit. "That's Deputy Randy Williamson. He's out on a property damage accident on Popcorn Road."

Even though she'd never been in a squad car, when she heard a police call on the radio, she concentrated on the nature of the policeman's mission and she would try to visualize the activity that ensued. One night when six Indiana University basketball fans returning to Bloomington after an away game were killed in the fiery crash of their plane, she listened to police traffic about it until 2:30 in the morning.

"It's my whole world," she said of the radio. "I didn't know what was going on until I got this radio."

She kept abreast of so much that neighbors would ring her bedside telephone to learn what was happening when they heard the sound of a siren. She was always pleased to accommodate them. One night, she heard the Morgan County sheriff's dispatcher order a squad car to the scene of a UFO sighting. The location sounded familiar. Betty twisted around in her bed so that she could look out the east window of her bedroom and there, hanging almost within reach, was the UFO – a huge balloon of rising orange moon.

Betty laughed at the recollection. "If people would just stop to think, they wouldn't do such silly things," she said.

The east window provided her with small pleasures. By her own count, a large birdfeeder, placed close to the window by her parents, had been host one fall and winter to as many as twenty-three different species of birds. During our visit an aggressive Cardinal attacked his reflection in the glass. Betty was amused. "Sometimes he'll go around to the south window," she said.

By twisting her body she could, with binoculars, scan the skies of all seasons to watch the clouds float by, or an airplane fly past overhead, or a helicopter, or to study the stars or the moon in a clear nighttime sky. From that twisted position, she could also watch the roadway that ran past her window.

"I like to watch the big trucks go by," she told me. "Oh," she once exclaimed with a smile, "driving one of those big diesel rigs sounds like fun to me. I love the sound of their motors, the sound of their air horns."

At that time "Movin' On", a weekly Thursday night television show starring Bedford, Indiana, native Claude Aikins was popular. It was Betty's favorite show and she watched it religiously on a small portable black and white television set.

Outside her east window, snow flurries whirled crazily before a fierce early April wind. As it had many times before, the first full moon after March 21 had arrived too soon. But there was no way to move the moveable feast of Easter to warmer more spring-like weather.

"This weather will keep your Easter Sunday visitors away," I said to Betty while gesturing toward the east window.

"I don't expect any visitors," she smiled from her bed. "I'm used to it," she continued. "Almost all my days are without visitors."

I was so moved by her courage in what I saw as a hopeless bedfast solitary confinement that I wrote a column about her in which I referred to her as "My Easter Girl." Soon afterward, Betty's world changed.

Moved by her courage, Bloomington city firemen purchased a multi-channel police scanner, delivered it personally to her home, and installed it in her bedroom within easy reach. She not only was able to receive clearer police calls then, but she was able to monitor several police departments, including state, county, and city, plus the city fire department.

47

Policemen, also attracted by what they read, provided her with copies of the 10-Code. She listened and learned cruiser numbers and could associate them with their drivers, and she learned to know policemen from the sound of their radio voices. Accidents, fires, ambulance runs, Signal 10 red light and siren runs of any kind, Betty vicariously rode to them all, in spirit at the side of the policemen.

"It's like being right there with them," she told me during another of our visits.

It was indeed a new world for her. A world of life and living and love. Love of police work. Love of the thin blue line itself. Love of each policeman as she heard them on the scanner in their work, in their play-acting she saw on television. And finally, it was a love as she dreamed it in the privacy of her own personal fantasies.

"If I could," she told me once, "I'd be a policeman."

After reading in my newspaper column about Betty and her little black and white portable television set, Viola Edwards, a lady in Mitchell, Indiana, was moved to make another change in Betty's world. Mrs. Edwards said, "My heart goes out to that girl. She ought to have a color television." She then picked up a hat, tossed a greenback into it and said, "Here's my ten. Who else?"

Mrs. Edwards was working at Wigley's Service Station on State Road 60, which was owned by her son. When word about what she'd started with the hat got out, people began sending her one and two and five dollars, and ten dollars, along with complimentary notes.

"God bless you," some said.

"It's so nice of you to take the time to do this," said one.

"It's nice of you to do this. I only hope and pray you get enough," said another.

Between the donations and a special factory price made available by RCA in Bloomington, she soon had enough. And one afternoon State Trooper Omar (Pete) Davis, who tooted his cruiser's horn every time he drove past Betty's house, and Lt. Robert Kirk, then commander of the Indiana State Police Post at Bloomington, picked up the new color television and delivered it to Betty's bedroom and installed it at the foot of her bed.

During the years of our acquaintance, I wrote a number of columns about Betty – "My Easter Girl." Some appeared before Easter Sunday. Some on Easter Sunday. Unfailingly, several days afterward, a letter would arrive from her.

"This is to say thank you to your many readers," she would write. And she would recount pleasure she derived from the visitors, the cards, the letters and the gifts that had arrived. Sometimes she would include a list of the names of those who wrote or visited her.

Gretchen Wayland, Bloomfield; Anna Bell Buskirk, Bloomington; Doris Logsden, Bedford; Betsy Mouton, Naples, Florida; Betty Hackney, Orleans; Dorothy Martin, Heltonville; and Marybeth Carney, Fort Wayne, are just a few of whose addresses give an indication of her widespread popularity.

And, in each letter to me, there was included a word about a special visitor, a policeman, carrying a gift. It might have been Trooper Davis. Another time Deputy Jerry Reed. Or Sheriff's Major Jimmy Young, Deputy Dick Allen, Deputy Jim Inman, Sheriff Bill Brown, Sheriff Randy Williamson. Deputy Larry Todd, Bloomington Fire Chief Richard Gose and Battalion Chief Don Oard.

There were others, many others, who came in response to Betty's courage and what they read about her. I remember that while I was writing one Easter Sunday column about her, Russ Parker and Lloyd Mosier were even then installing at Betty's bedside a CB base radio, another gift to her from Bloomington city firemen. They wanted her to have some means other than her telephone to make contact with the outside world. She loved it. And guess what name she chose for her CB "handle?" You're right – "Easter Girl."

After my last visit with her, I wrote that it required a great deal of bravery and self discipline to prevail in a physical world as tiny and limited as Betty's. And I noted that she had become an inspiration to untold scores of people. The next time we visited, she denied any special power to overcome her situation.

"Sometimes," she admitted, "I feel sorry for myself. But I do try not to. I do try to block out self pity and think of something more interesting. I try to take each day as it comes, and I find that they are like everybody else's days – some are good and some are bad, and some are pretty good and some are pretty bad."

During my first visit to her bedside, I had inquired of her plans for the coming Easter Sunday. Easter Sunday, she replied, was unimpressive, just another boring day among many boring days.

She said she believed in the miracle of Easter, but added, "At times it's very hard to do."

When last I saw her, she spoke enthusiastically of a visit from Sammy Freeman, minister of the Friendship Separate Baptist Church, and some members of his congregation, and of a visit from George Fair of the Salem Church in Owen County, and I was aware of a change in her attitude. It was Eastertime again, and I again asked her view of the season, and of Easter Sunday.

"Since you started writing about me," she said, "it's a sort of enjoyable day now. It's sort of a day to look forward to."

She smiled and added, "The mailman says we get more mail than anyone else on his route. I just love to get cards and letters."

In its way, life for Betty was just as real as it was for anyone else, maybe more, and there was no denying how limited hers was. On the eve of a birthday anniversary when I asked her plans for the future her mood was somewhat depressed.

"I don't have much to look forward to," she said touchingly, candidly. "No dreams. No hopes. I gave all that up years ago." The wisp of a smile touched her mouth. "I've accepted it," she said. A moment later she added, "I don't say much about it, but I get awful lonesome at times."

Before I left that day, Betty smiled and said, "Have a happy Easter, again." Then, with a ring of what I took to be satisfaction in her voice, she said, "I've got just about everything I can think of. And I've got the world partly by the tail."

Her ordeal over at last, Betty, on her last day on earth, lay in an oak casket attired in a green frock she had selected from an advertisement in a catalog.

"She loved that dress; she thought it was so pretty," her mother recalled. "It had embroidery and gold braid on it."

The favorite dress was almost completely hidden by a gold blanket, a promise Betty had elicited long before her death from her mother that she would go to her eternal rest tucked under a gold blanket.

Two Monroe County sheriff's cruisers led her funeral procession to the cemetery. Another followed the last car. At the cemetery, six uniformed deputies and Sheriff Randy Williamson carried her to her grave.

Later, after enumerating the many condolences, the floral pieces, the kind words, Betty's mother said, "We appreciate so much everything that everyone has done for her." A thought occurred to her and Helen Fox added, "And Betty does, too."

JOSEPH

Hands clasped behind his head, he lounged comfortably at one end of the living room couch. One bare foot was pulled up under a thigh while the other stretched to the surface of a coffee table. There it rocked on a heel from side to side in measured cadence with his words.

As he spoke, the corners of his mouth alternately pulled back and flicked upwards in a spatter of thin, flashing smiles, movements matched by his mobile clear blue eyes. Though far from being one, on this September afternoon in 1970, he appeared for all the world as a teenager filled with a zest for life and living. His thoughts were about life – his ambition, he said, was to live to be one hundred years old. He offered little reason to doubt he would make it. Evidence that he might exuded from him in waves of confidence.

Longevity in his family had been a fact. The promised three-score and ten-plus star had shone down upon them with the brilliance and certainty of the rising sun. Now, twenty-four years past the fulfillment of the biblical promise, Joseph H. Haseman, ex-Boy Scout, ex-scoutmaster, ex-school teacher, ex-school superintendent, ex-so many things, was aiming for the merit badge of merit badges. To aid this youthful, old, happy man in that quest, kin and kind from as far away as California had gathered at a belated Sunday birthday party to wish him Godspeed and continued health to that end.

The saga of Joseph H. Haseman, who was born August 27, 1876, and who lived at 59 Fifth St. NE, in Linton, cannot be told in a few words. Yet there are those highlights in the lives of some men that attract notice and bring light and meaning to the lives of others, bright happenings of a lifetime that stand out as departures from the commonplace, that can be and should be told.

After twenty-three years as a teacher and administrator in the Linton School System, Joseph retired in 1918. That same year Beatrice Steward, a girl who was later to play a major role in his life, entered her freshman year at Linton High School.

At fifty-two, Joseph could have retired and rocked his way into old age. Instead, he became secretary-treasurer in the Linton Trust Company. He held that position until the bank moratorium of 1933 and the beginning of the Great Depression. It was in that year, too, that he was appointed agent of the state of Indiana to liquidate a bank at Shelbyville.

An incident five years earlier had also affected that year, making it perhaps a most memorable one of his long life. At a church meeting he met the girl who was a high school freshman in 1918, the year he retired from teaching. Their acquaintance grew into friendship, and that into courtship. On September 3, 1933, they married; he was fifty-seven, Beatrice Steward was thirty years younger.

"I used to be so scared of him when he was superintendent," she recalled her early school years. "I used to walk a block out of my way to avoid him."

Such was the childish awe in which school administrators of that period were held. At this time, however, with the benefit of experience and hindsight, she attributed the success of their marriage, which included three married children, and six grandchildren, to a lesser god, one endowed, she said, of great patience, understanding, and love.

They also had similar backgrounds. Each had grown up in the country. He was the oldest of nine children, she the oldest of four. Each was the sum of a period that held marriage and family paramount in its ambition. He was a teacher, and for thirty-four years she also taught in the Linton Stockton School Corporation.

Looking back on their years together, Joseph's eyes twinkled brightly with recollection. "We've never even had a fight," he laughed. Then in mock sorrow he made a face and added, "We've never even had a spat."

A recollection from the early years of their marriage involved their children. "Each of them had a morning newspaper home delivery route," Joseph began the account with obvious and understandable pride. "We'd get up at four o'clock in the morning, the five of us, and we'd deliver newspapers."

"Yes," said Beatrice, equally proud. "We covered this whole town, and it was a lot of hard work. But when our children were ready for college, each of them had two thousand dollars in the bank."

"All from delivering newspapers, too," said Joseph. "They put every nickel in the bank."

Papers sold for a nickel then. Joseph Jr.'s nickels helped him to become a pharmacist. Beatrice Ann and James used theirs to follow in the footsteps of their parents and became teachers.

Although longevity may be hereditary, Joseph did not deny the fact that he had remained active all his life; involvement in Red Cross, Odd Fellows, Masonry, other fraternal orders, and church, besides everything else. And at ninety-four, he was still active, despite failing eyesight and the support of a quad-cane.

"I believe what has helped keep me young is that I've always given to young people — my time, my efforts, my respect," said Joseph. "I like them, and I get along with them very well."

His mother-in-law, Mrs. Mary Steward, who had been listening quietly, spoke up for the first time. "I agree," she smiled. "I get along with him just fine. I have no complaints against him." Mary Steward was ninety-one.

After a moment of laughter Joseph became serious. "Age," he said, "is no recommendation, no basis, for marriage. If a man marries a girl and takes good care of her, and becomes a good family man, why, they just have to be happy and successful."

FLOSSIE

They grew lush and beautiful and neighbors sometimes stopped in passing to comment on Flossie Tolbert's gardens.

"I never saw anybody throw down stuff and it just takes off like it does for you," a neighbor told Flossie one day.

Another said, "I never seen so much garden raised with a hoe."

Flossie had two gardens where she lived on a curve of Indiana 450 between Dover Hill and State Road 54 near Shoals. They flanked her small house which was shaded by maple trees. It was an old house. The outbuildings also were old, and were blanketed with vines. The T-posts that held up her sagging clotheslines were tilted from time and stress. And time and stress had aged Flossie. But the gardens were new, and they showed signs of affectionate care.

"I do it all with a hoe," Flossie said proudly as she leaned heavily on the long handle of that garden tool.

It was hot and humid and the brim of an ancient blue bonnet she wore to protect her head from a bright sun came down so low it almost hid Flossie's face. Her sneakered feet and ankles were visible below the hem of a long patched dress. She wore an over-sized man's long-sleeve, faded, blue denim shirt

FLOSSIE TOLBERT

over that, unbuttoned. A tiny woman, she looked almost swallowed up in her clothes. A nearby faceless scarecrow, by comparison, appeared large, robust.

"I love to hoe," she smiled, showing a gold tooth. "I can hoe better than I can do anything else. And I'm awfully proud of my stuff."

Her stuff consisted of burpless cucumbers, tomatoes, mangoes, cabbages, beets, peas, squash, green beans — everything that usually grew in a vegetable garden, plus sweet potatoes.

"I get out real early," she explained her success with the primitive tool. "I'm ashamed to say it, but I just love to hoe in the garden. Here I am, eighty-one years old, still just a-beatin' and a-thumpin'."

Up in the day, Flossie would stop work to go into the house to rest. Toward evening she'd return to the gardens to beat and thump with the hoe some more. Despite her best efforts, weeds and foxtails, nourished by rains, abounded. Still, her crops flourished.

"I'm too old to cut the mustard," Flossie admitted, "but my gardens make those young people ashamed of themselves, I'll tell you. I've got the best beets. They're so pretty, and the cabbages are so nice, and the mangoes. I put out my gardens the first of May, and I work in them. That's the difference."

Flossie lived alone. Her husband, Alus, had died six years earlier at age eighty-five, after they had been married fifty-nine years. He was blind the last seven years of his life. They had two sons, one of whom was killed in an auto accident in 1950. The other visited his mother regularly. A nephew lived close.

"I try to be happy," Flossie said after recounting the tragedy that took her son's life. "I don't let myself get lonely. I was at first, but you have to go ahead. I can't live in the past all the time. I know I've got to keep a-goin.' "

Weeds and foxtails were not the only unwelcome visitors to Flossie's gardens. Deer came there, too, to dine on her sweet potatoes.

"That's what that scarecrow is there for, but it doesn't bother them," she said. "I'll see one and I'll come out and holler at it and it'll just stand there and look at me. It makes me so mad."

She was obviously chagrined at the memory.

"The deer like them, they're so good," she said of her sweet potatoes. "If you eat any of them, you'll never like the others. They're purple sweet potatoes. They are the sweetest things. And those Nancy Halls – good? Are they! If I didn't have them, I'd never put out a sweet potato," she said.

What the deer didn't get, Flossie gave to her neighbors and friends; sweet potatoes and the various yields of her gardens.

"I do can some but I'm not goin' to can a heck of a lot this year," she vowed. "I'll can beets, for sure. I love beets. And relish and stuffed mangoes. They're so good."

Flossie put the hoe aside.

"You've caught me in my worst dress, but it's my coolest," she said. "But I want you to take some burpless cucumbers with you, and some tomatoes, and some mangoes."

She picked up a long stick to serve as a cane and started through an opening in a wire fence that was thickly woven with rich pink sweet peas.

"You wait here and I'll run down and see if I can find you some, honey," she said.

She did, of course. But she did not run.

One February day almost four years later, I stopped to see Flossie again just to say hello. She was delighted to see me. I have learned in my travels that elderly people are always glad to have someone visit, almost anyone, even a nosy newspaper reporter. They seem always to be lonesome.

The few years that had passed since my first visit with her had left their mark on Flossie. On me, too, I'm sure, but we rarely see the changes in ourselves. But Flossie's spirit was as young as ever.

"The good Lord willing," she smiled, "I'll put out a garden this spring, in May."

It was a great day for thinking about gardens. A bright sun shone down from a cloudless sky and, except for a snaggle-tooth bite to a waning winter wind, the temperature outdoors was comfortably bearable.

Just to be sure she would not be cold, Flossie had wrapped her ninety-eight pounds in a full-length black coat, under which she wore a red flannel shirt, and slacks and galoshes. She had a crocheted gold hat on her head, a powder blue babushka over that and tied under her chin, and a white scarf around her neck. Her tiny hands, one of which grasped a long, slightly bent stick, and the other which supported her weight on a metal quad-cane that glittered in the sunlight, seemed lost in oversized brown jersey gloves.

"I bought three packages of cucumber seeds the other day," she said. "I already got lettuce seed and all kinds of tomato seeds. But I usually buy tomato plants, they're healthier and do better. Last year I had the earliest tomatoes of anybody around."

Despite her readiness to start planting, it occurred to me that the good Lord, in addition to being willing, might have to lend her his support. For in deference to the loyal long stick, and the shiny quad cane that shared the burden of keeping Flossie on her feet, she had other problems. Not the least of which was her age, which by then had increased to eighty-five.

Still, she was determined to challenge the furrows. And to make the job easier, for herself and the Lord, she planned to set out only one of her usual two gardens. She also expressed a willingness to accept more assistance from her son, Alus Ray, who lived in Indianapolis and still visited his mother regularly to help her around the house and yard.

"He's awfully afraid that I shouldn't work, that I will fall. But if I can lift a hoe – I love to hoe – I'll hoe. But if I can't, I tell him, I'll do the bossin'," she said.

Flossie's mailbox was on the opposite side of the highway from her house on a dangerous curve. She had hoped for years to have it moved to her side of the road. That she had survived the daily crossings to pick up her mail the past four years, in spite of her aging, led me to believe the good Lord had assigned a guardian angel to be her crossing guard.

Neighbor Hattie Henry who lived over the hill from Flossie's was a big help in that respect. When mail person Charles (Bob) Brunner, passed her house and headed in the direction of Flossie's, Hattie would call Flossie on the telephone. That kept her from making needless trips across the highway to the mailbox. It also gave her time to dress for the weather, and to psych herself up to brave one more crossing of that dangerous curve.

"It's a shame that I can't have that mailbox on this side of the road," she said. "But if I did, I'd always be afraid that Bob would get hit bringing me the mail. If he did, I think I'd die. He's such a nice person."

Flossie's life, to hear her tell it, was filled with nice persons. Their names fell from her lips like shining stars.

"Bob Brett, he's retired from the post office. He's such a nice person, and he helps me. And Hattie. She sees that I don't go hungry (Hattie took Flossie shopping). And when it's slick, she comes to get my mail out of the box for me. She's better to me than a sister. And the Diamonds, Patsy and Darrell, they brought me my Thanksgiving and Christmas dinners. You name it and they had it for me. And Lester Padgett, from over at Bramble. He brought me seventy-five to a hundred dollars worth of food at Christmas; him and his wife, Delores.

"I'll tell you right now," she shook her head for emphasis, "you'll never be around any better people. And friends like Wilson and Joyce Downs. Anything I have to do, they do it. The other day she just jumped right in and carried three or four armloads of wood into the house for me. Somebody's always carrying wood in for me."

Flossie was a good neighbor, too. And a fine woman. Until his death, she was devoted to her husband. During the last eight years of his life, after the surgical removal of his eyes due to advanced glaucoma, she saw to his every need, "and raised a garden every year, too," she said.

Now she was looking forward to spring and another garden. It would not be easy. Flossie had some physical problems. A year after my first visit with her, she had fallen and fractured a hip, and had arthritis in her back, "And," as she described their affect on her, "they left me all drawed up. But," she hurried to add, "I'll be out there hoeing if I'm alive. And," she smiled hopefully, "my doctor, Larry Sutton, said he's going to do everything he can to keep me that way."

Age took its gradual toll on Flossie. There came a time when she could no longer care for herself, and she went to live with her son. We corresponded a couple of times. Then one day late in 1994 I was informed that she was in a nursing home in Loogootee and I promised myself to visit her there.

I very nearly did. As I was leaving Shoals one day, I thought I would return to Bloomington via a route that would take me through Loogootee, which I had taken many times. But for some reason I turned in the other direction, on U.S. 50 east out of Shoals. After I did so I told myself, "I'll visit Flossie another day."

I didn't get the chance. A short time later I was surprised to see Flossie's name in the obituary column of the daily newspaper. I am still disturbed, probably always will be, by my decision to put off my visit to her.

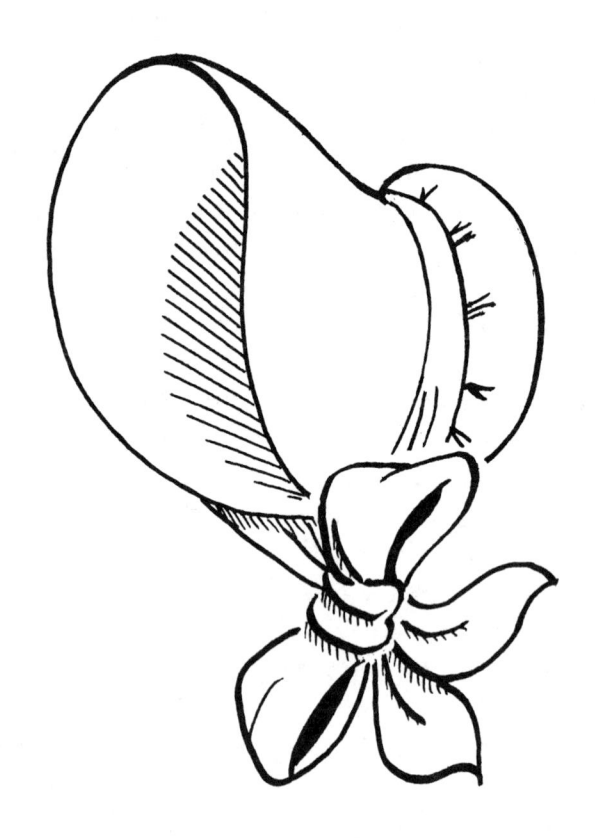

DRESDEN DAYS

It was an event to walk to George O'Bannon's store to spend a nickel for a bottle of cool soda pop. Although there were no electric refrigerators then, O'Bannon had a dug-well in the back room and, in a bucket at the end of a rope in the cool water therein, he kept a supply of refreshing soft drinks.

"It was worth the nickel just to watch him pull the rope and see the bucket full of dripping bottles come up," Helen Wright of Bloomfield, remembered.

O'Bannon's store was in Dresden, a town whose disappearance coincided with the arrival of such newfangled gadgets as refrigerators. Unless a stranger were led by a former resident to its site, it probably could not be found.

"There are a few trailers there," Jasper Wright tried to help. "But if you go too far, there are some more trailers."

Once a thriving rural center – the store, Waggoner & Quimby Blacksmith Shop, a grist mill, post office and railroad station – Dresden was situated on the old Bloomfield-Owensburg road.

"There were times," Helen continued with her recollection, "when there'd be others in the store who wanted a soda pop, and they'd just wait around until George pulled that bucket up to get theirs."

O'Bannon's and the smithy were social centers. When the men could not be in the fields due to inclement weather, they were at one or the other of those places. After the Waggoner & Quimby establishment burned, Quimby – Ernest "Bump" Quimby – and Richard Merritt opened another smithy.

In the interim, O'Bannon's was the pulse of Dresden. Candy sticks were two for a penny and O'Bannon kept a board game for the amusement of his customers. O'Bannon's wife, Mary, helped in the store and was remembered by Helen as "a good soul."

They had a son, Charlie, who wanted to be a railroad locomotive engineer. After firing on the Monon for some years, Charlie O'Bannon got his wish. And after that, when the Monon's "Old Nellie" steam locomotive huffed and puffed toward Dresden, Charlie would lean on its whistle.

"Oh, he'd just blow and blow that thing," Helen recalled. "He'd always wanted to be an engineer, and he never let Dresden forget he'd become one."

Jasper, then eighty-two, remembered meal time in Dresden. Wagons were lined up and down the main road with horses hitched to fence posts, as folks waited to have their corn ground at the mill.

"If there was only one person and he had to have it, they'd grind for one," Jasper said. "But usually they'd wait until there were several people. Then they'd grind. They'd call that meal time. I remember how they'd grind a little, scoop up a handful and show it to the customer and ask, 'Is that about right?' They'd grind it however you wanted it."

Quimby usually assisted with the grinding. A friendly, smiling man, he had been handicapped from childhood. As a result, he walked with the aid of a metal-tipped cane that went bump-bump-bump as he walked. Hence the nickname Bump.

"He never minded," Helen said. "He was a wonderful person. He was a tinkerer. He could fix anything, and he used to fix watches and clocks."

Helen and Jasper remembered a few of their teachers at Dresden School: L. D. "Dow" Hudson, Leonard George and Oscar Boruff, who taught in the days when a field trip was to a nearby haunted house.

"Oscar took us," Jasper said. "It was supposed to be haunted. While we were in the place, I stayed close to where he was."

In later years, Jasper drove for Kraft-Phoenix and picked up milk at farms around Springville, Owensburg, Doan, Scotland and Bloomfield. His truck was also the only motor transportation around, and he'd haul people free of charge from one place to another. Once he drove into Bloomfield with thirteen passengers on board.

Kraft-Phoenix made cheese at Bloomfield. From 1928 to 1942, when he left his job there, Jasper drove a number of different trucks. One was put together for him by Helen's brother, Charles Records. "It had a Dodge front and a Ford back end," Jasper described it.

Jasper left Dresden in 1922, and Helen left there when she married him three years later. At this time, they were nearing their fifty-eighth anniversary. They had four children and seven grandchildren.

The Wrights took pride in a number of things, including earning their own living all their lives. Jasper always had a job, had never had to work on WPA and they'd never been on welfare. Dresden was a good training ground for that kind of independence; one made it on what he could earn and what he could grow, and that was that, Jasper said.

"I miss Dresden," Helen said. "I lay awake at night sometimes and I can see inside the old schoolhouse; the map box; the little bookcase we were so proud of;

the nails from which we hung our coats; the shelf for our lunches; and the shelf that held the cedar water bucket with the dipper inside. I see everything, including the potbellied stove, where I sat, where the teacher sat. I get lonely for all of it," she said.

Jasper and Helen had always been told that a black man named Dan (last name unknown) plotted Dresden, arranging streets and lots in the manner of towns of that period. He and his wife, Mary, are believed to be buried at Ashcraft Chapel, not too distant from the site of the community.

Helen's father and mother, Butler and Laura Records, are also buried there. Laura's uncle, Joseph Ashcraft, donated the ground for the cemetery. Jasper's parents, Albert and Ada Wright, are interred at Flynn Cemetery.

If there were no nickel fares to pick up at the depot when he guided Old Nellie into Dresden, Charlie O'Bannon would ease back on the throttle and slow the train down enough for station agent Aleck Boyer to toss the mail bag on board. Then Charlie would lean on that whistle and steam off. It was a sight to see and a joy to hear, Helen said.

OLD - NELLIE

TAYLOR WILSON

Taylor Wilson had big plans for his retirement. He furnished a garage workshop at his Christiansburg Road home in Brown County with woodworking machinery and tools with which he planned to fashion wood furniture and wood curios. And why not? He had this love affair going with wood; turned a lovely chair on his lathe; cut and put together a handsome sassafras desk; made picture frames; designed, constructed and installed his own kitchen cabinets.

Alas. Arthritis struck his hands. It left them twisted and turned. Finally, in the right one, surgeons implanted plastic and stainless steel knuckles. And Taylor Wilson sold the machinery and tools in his garage workshop.

"But it's always pleasant living around here," he said taking a compensatory view of his misfortune as we sat in the living room of his home. "I was born in this house, and I've seen progress come to this place, and it's been good."

Progress came in the form of a better road, electric lights, and municipal water.

"I can remember when for three months out of the year you couldn't get a Model-T Ford out of here," he said.

His mother, Amanda Deaver, lived until she was ninety-eight, and she saw all the improvements except the installation of the water lines. The water was purchased by the Southeastern Brown County Water Corporation.

Amanda Deaver was born on Weed Patch Hill, about four miles northwest of the Wilson home, as the crow flies. The community was then known as Kelp, and Wilson remembered his mother recounting the manner in which they lived: simply, from their own gardens, their own sorghum cane, their own maple trees. They ate breakfast, dinner and supper, then, and homemade biscuits were as common to the table as were the potatoes, beans, cornbread and kraut which they ate almost daily.

"I remember my mother telling how her mother used to go out to the kraut barrel in the winter time and chop a wedge of it out and bring it in and cook it. They kept a hatchet out by the barrel to chop the frozen kraut with," Wilson said.

Christiansburg School was about a mile and one-half down the road, and it provided Wilson with his entire formal education.

"I trotted out there for twelve years," he recalled. During his last four years there he played basketball. "We played Houston, Courtland, Freetown, Nashville, Helmsburg and Clearspring, and every year we played in the Franklin tourney. I remember that one year there were only thirteen of us enrolled in the high school, and eight of those were boys. And another year there were only five of us to go to the Franklin tourney, so we took a freshman boy who had never played ball, just so we would have six players there," he said.

William Marion Allen was both principal of the school and the basketball coach. Christiansburg failed to win any of the tournaments in Wilson's four years as a member of the squad, and they won few of their regular games, he said.

The Wilson home was a short ride southwest of Pikes Peak, and, as was much of that area, it was situated within the R. 6, Columbus mail course.

Several years ago, Wilson had clipped a series of Arthur Singer's bird prints and flowers from the pages of the American Home Magazine, and, while he was still able, he cut out and grooved frames for them, and they hung on the flower-pattern wallpaper walls of the living room of his home. They were a gorgeous collection that warmed an already friendly room. One group surrounded an interesting old print in one of those ancient, gilded curlicue frames.

"My parents lived in a house back up the hill here before they built this one," Wilson recounted the history of that print, a small child seated by an unusually large dog. "Peddlers used to come through here then and my mother liked it so well she gave one fifty-cents for it. When my father came in and saw it he raised the devil 'cause she spent fifty-cents from the money they were saving to build this house."

The Wilsons went to church at New Bellsville, east of Pikes Peak and several miles from the Wilson home. The Harmony Baptist Church, it was then, and still was at this time. In the early days, New Bellsville was a busy little community, but when I called at Taylor Wilson's, just a few homes, a couple of tumble-down buildings, the well-maintained church, and a cemetery that sloped down to the road were the only components of life there. Wilson's parents and several other relatives were buried there.

When his interest turned from the workshop to genealogy, Wilson learned that Phillip King Jr., a relative on his mother's side, was a Revolutionary War soldier, and that he was born in Somerset County, Pennsylvania. His maternal grandmother was a Skinner, and he recalled that his mother used to tell him that her mother came from the Alleghenies. When they reached the Ohio River, they took a boat down to Madison, Indiana, and from there her family took a train to Columbus.

"They came from Columbus to here in a wagon," Wilson said.

His construction of the family tree was to reveal that the "Alleghenies" to which his grandmother referred was a mountain district known as Turkey Foot, which also was in Somerset County, Pennsylvania. And he later learned that the Skinner family began its westward trek from Woodbridge, New Jersey.

His great grandfather, Dr. Samuel Wilson, practiced medicine in the general area of the Wilson home, and the remains of his journal, from 1873-1877 was in Wilson's possession. He also had a number of old medicine books which were Dr. Wilson's; *King's New American Family Physician*, dated 1860, was one of them.

Among the more than a thousand pages of that book we found sections devoted to all manner of ailments, among which were treatments for milk leg, fainting fits, weakness in the back, milk fever, white thrush, wind colic, summer complaint, warts, corns, and bunions, and "what young girls should know."

CRAIG PETERS

Craig Peters ticked off the names: "Albert Skirvin, Noble Sciscoe, Clifford Kinser, Bud Duncan, Clifford Thrasher, Bill Brown. That," she said proudly, "is a record."

Record indeed: a twenty-eight year record of service to the six Monroe County sheriffs whom she named, and to the residents of Monroe County.

"And," she said during my visit to her courthouse office one day, "I have loved it."

She planned to leave it all in exchange for a quasi-private life she planned to share between her Bloomington home and, she said, "Those who I have neglected all these years; those folks in nursing homes, in hospitals, and the shut-ins. I want to comfort them."

As a pretty teenager, Craig arrived in Bloomington from Harrodsburg, where she was born, and where she graduated from high school. At that early age, she was already a popular singer, having sung at funerals around the county since she was about seven. It was as a singer that she also achieved another record; she had sung at 6,686 funerals.

"I began singing before I could walk," she smiled at the recollection. "Since I started singing at funerals I've sung in Sullivan, Marion, Greene, Lawrence, Owen, Brown, Washington, Jackson, Orange, Clinton and Morgan counties.

CRAIG PETERS
The Early Days

"Lots of times," she said, "I'd sing at three and four funerals a day – that was during the big flu epidemic before the Twenties. That was when we'd have to stand out on the porch and sing, because we weren't allowed in the houses where the killer influenza disease had been."

If the weather could possibly turn bad in time for a funeral, it usually did, adding many discomforts to the life of service she had chosen.

"We'd drive to those homes we could get to," she said of herself and her many singing companions through the years. "Funerals were held in homes back then. When we couldn't reach them we'd ride in the hearse with the undertaker, and the deceased. Several times we had to ride in a horse-drawn wagon; the going on the way to a cemetery would be too rough for a hearse."

At some of those funerals, she witnessed some minor tragedies; a mourner jumped into the grave atop a casket; a woman flung herself on a corpse and the casket lid came down on her.

Some incidents were not without humor. At a country church funeral, a daughter of the deceased insisted that Craig and Ygonda "Bake" Henderson should sing three verses someone had scribbled on a piece of blank paper.

"There was no music with them," Craig remembered. "But this woman wanted us to sing them. So Bake and I went out behind the church and shut ourselves in the privy, where we practiced trying to put music to those words."

During the service, the three verses came out as unlike in tune as though they were three different songs. Yet after the service, the daughter of the dead man complimented the two singers.

"She said, 'That was wonderful. You sang it just exactly right. That was just exactly what Paw wanted.' " Craig recalled the woman's words.

Bake died in 1951 and Craig was joined in the funeral duets by Mae Patton. Others with whom she sang in the achievement of this second record included Judge Donald Rogers, Bill Curry, Bill Griffin, Tom Duncan, "all the Isoms from Hendricksville," Martin and Lew Brock and Keith Chitwood. Quartets in which she sang included Stella Burch, Nina Baker and Josephine Ranard.

Another companion in song was Craig's own daughter, Martha Jean Agnew. When she died in 1973, Craig stopped singing.

"I've been called to sing," she said, "but I just can't sing anymore."

A year prior to Martha's death, her father, Leslie L. "Pete" Peters, Craig's husband, died. Pete had barbered at three different locations on Courthouse Square and was well-known in Bloomington.

"But I have friends," she said bittersweetly of the loss of her family. "I made them by the hundreds when I was singing, and here in the courthouse. The attorneys – they come in every day with papers. I could name them, but I'm afraid I might leave one out by accident and that wouldn't be right. And all the people in the sheriff's department."

To say farewell to her co-workers as easily as possible, Craig had prepared a missive which she planned to send to those her office served.

"I have been mighty happy in my work," it read in part. "And I am most grateful for everything you have done for me, even when sadness came . . . the years of service to the sheriff's department, the many funerals at which I sang, now will be tucked away in precious memories . . . "

She was anxious to return to private life. She welcomed the challenges of it as calmly as she did a wintertime pulpit left empty by a snowbound minister. "We'll conduct this funeral ourselves," she told the funeral director. And the service went off without a hitch.

Looking forward to retirement, she said, "I'll be happy to go to those I've neglected – I'm going to put in my time visiting them in nursing homes, and at their homes."

After Craig graduated from the eighth grade at Harrodsburg and moved to Bloomington, the old school burned down. My suggestion that it sounded like an indictment against her gave her a laugh. It wasn't, really. Those events just happened to come one after the other.

"I was born there," Craig said of Harrodsburg and of the school she remembered, "I used to play the organ there every day, when the kids marched in."

After moving to Bloomington, she enrolled at Bloomington High School, the site now occupied by Seminary Square at Second and Walnut Streets, and later studied voice for four years at the Indiana University School of Music. We talked at length about her voice, including the many times it had been heard at funerals.

"I have so many favorite songs," she responded to a question about her favorite of those she'd sung over the years. "I just don't know how I could possibly pick just one of them."

Suddenly remembering something, she tilted her silver-gray head a bit, and said, "I don't want any singing at my funeral, I just want the words to songs read."

Then she winked and laughed, and she said, "They might just get a bad singer in, and I wouldn't like that."

But her fear of a bad singer slipping into that role at her funeral must have been real for she said in a more serious vein, "I want the words to about a dozen songs of the many songs I've sung, read, and I will pick them out in time, and I'll give them to somebody."

In addition to the ban on singing, Craig also banned praise and glory from her funeral. "The Lord knows me and what I have done in this life," she said, "and that'll be sufficient. But I do want one or two tears, and I hope I'll leave some precious memories behind with friends."

Among the many chapters in her life that had become so familiar to the Lord, I hope this brief one that I have written here about Craig will someday be included. It's not much, yet it is a bit of biography about a lovely lady.

Deputy Sheriff Craig Peters — that was her official job title. At the time we talked she was employed by Monroe County Sheriff Bill Brown, the sixth and last sheriff for whom she conducted official business.

She began with Albert Skirvin in 1943, and she remained with Al for two two-year terms through 1946. Two similar terms were spent with Noble Sciscoe, from 1947 through 1950. When Fred Davis won that office for one four-year term, in 1951, Craig was employed elsewhere. She returned when Clifford Kinser became sheriff in 1955 and stayed with him through two terms. Her next sheriff was Bud Duncan, in 1963, and she stayed with him for one year. She again returned in 1967 when Clifford Thrasher became sheriff. And was there for Bill Brown's first term.

Craig dressed immaculately, and wore her pretty hair in a braided bun on the back of her head. Atop the bun she placed colorful Spanish combs and around her neck she wore multiple long necklaces of bright beads. Earrings, too, were a standard part of her accessories. She was simply lovely in her daily appearance.

Craig had always been attractive. Once, many years before I met her, when she was working for The Wicks Company, Inc., on Sixth Street, on Bloomington's Courthouse Square, she was in a big show window arranging ladies' clothing on a mannequin. A young man riding on a bicycle was attracted to her, and while his eyes were fastened on her beauty, the bike slammed into two policemen, toppling them all to the ground.

"If you were looking at her," one of the policemen who knew Craig growled after regaining his feet, "we won't take you in."

The bicycle rider was Pete, who later became Craig's husband. Craig also had three sisters and a brother: Madonna Kutche, Dorothy Mellette, and Lois Isom, who lived in Bloomington, and Curt Young, whose home was in Muncie.

But for those times of sadness that came into her life, Craig said her years had been wonderful, and that given the opportunity to live them once again would not be temptation enough to induce her to change a single hour of them.

Sometime before she passed away, Martha handed me the following verse on a half sheet of typing paper. I held on to it through the years, really never quite knowing the reason why. When I prepared this recollection of her mother, I decided to use it in this space. I'm sure Craig would have found some satisfaction in that. I hope you do, too.

We are likened to the flowers – strong when new, weak when old.
Mankind reaches for the sunlight 'till the final chapter's told.
Oftentimes I think upon this, and I here and now confess
The prospect of being old sometimes fills me with distress.
Of course, I am well aware that pessimism isn't good
And I must be optimistic to enhance livelihood,
But I am a keen observer of the moving stage of life,
And even rose-colored glasses cannot hide its pain and strife.
So, with measured steps I journey, keeping faith in God on high,
So that when life's flower withers my new soul will never die.

– Martha Jean Agnew

'CLICK-CLICK'

It was blood chilling, hearing the old river bridge crack and bang like gunfire behind him. Had he not been fleet of foot, Henry Bough might not have been comfortably seated in his living room relating the experience. But he was just fast enough to stay ahead of the crumbling structure.

"Oh, gosh," he exclaimed at the memory, "talk about a noise! I ran. Oh, how I ran. I didn't look back until I got plumb off and clear."

When he did look back, Henry saw that the east end of the covered bridge that spanned the White River on Old Lyons Road south of Bloomfield had crashed down into the water.

There were other witnesses: the county bridge gang that Henry had arrived with to repair a crack in the floor of the long span, and Erwin Ramsey, an east bank farmer who was plowing corn near the bridge. Carrying a red flag, Henry had been dispatched on foot across the span to stop traffic while the repair was being made.

"As I started across, I heard a 'click-click' but I didn't pay much attention," Henry, a bald, spare man of seventy-eight with bright blue eyes, straightened in his chair at the memory. "Then I heard somebody holler, 'There she goes!' I didn't look back." He held his hands up and glanced one palm off the other. "I took out across that bridge with it cracking and banging behind me like guns.

"When I got across and looked back, the bridge was down in the river. It didn't float away. It stayed right there. I heard somebody holler, 'Oh, no! Where's Henry?' But I was all right. Somebody said, 'It ain't been ten minutes since I crossed that bridge.' And Johnny Stone and his wife and two children had just crossed ahead of me in their truck loaded with ashes," Henry said.

Erwin Ramsey was driving in the direction of the bridge when the east end of the span fell. "I just happened to be looking right at it," he said. "I heard the cracking noise and watched it go down."

Some twenty-three years had passed since the bridge had plunged into the river and the time I visited with Henry. He told me that he had just left his farm near Scotland to live in Bloomfield and to work on the Greene County bridge gang. He was born and reared in Taylor Township, one of nine children of Chris and Nancy Graham Bough. The change was a big one for him and his wife, Nellie Dove.

"But I worked six more years on that bridge gang," Henry said, "and I never had anything like that ever happen to me again. That once was enough."

Most countians will remember Henry best from the years he was custodian at the courthouse. When he first took the job, Commissioner Mark Sexton used to remind him, "Henry, if you don't like this job, just come back to the bridge gang." But Henry declined that offer each time it was made and stayed on the courthouse job for fourteen years.

Nellie Dove worked with him as the courthouse matron for five of those years, until she was stricken with leukemia. Twenty-six days later she was dead. Henry spent almost every day of the last fifteen days of her life at her bedside in Robert Long Hospital in Indianapolis. He remembered their last seconds together.

"She knew she was dying," he said, the words catching in his throat. "I kissed her goodbye and told her, 'I'll meet you in Heaven.' And she said, 'I'm ready to go. Kiss me again.' And she died right after."

Henry believed that he and his new wife, Dorothy, would both find their former mates in Heaven. Evidence of that faith abounded in the living room of their home: two well-worn Bibles; a sofa cushion with a Christian poem embroidered on it; a praying hands print; a Gethsemane print; and a print of Christ knocking on a closed door that could be opened only from the inside.

Henry and his brother, Jona, who was eighty years old and living with his wife, Rachel, near Hobbieville, were the only surviving members of the Bough family. Henry believed that when they got to Heaven, they'd find their brothers and sisters there, too. He believed in "the promise," he said.

He explained that the promise is pretty well stated throughout Chapter Ten of St. John: "I am the door . . . I am the good shepherd . . . My sheep hear my voice . . . I give them eternal life . . . I and my Father are one," he quoted from it.

"Sometimes," Henry gave another indication of his faith, "I sit and think about our many loved ones who have gone to Heaven, and about God and His promise, and I weep tears of joy," he said.

Henry Bough was not known as far and wide as some men. But he was about as well-liked and respected as any man could be by those who did know him. From the time he was old enough he always tried to give his best to his family, friends, his fellow man and his employers, and to his God. He always tried to do more than his share, such as when he'd push the rotary lawn mower from the courthouse to the county jail where he'd mow the lawn. Mowing the jail lawn wasn't his job, and he didn't get paid for doing it, but he did it anyway. When Dale Horn became sheriff, he relieved Henry of that job by having prisoners mow the lawn. But it was little things like that that endeared Henry to so many.

When I met Henry he had a couple of little jobs to supplement his and Dorothy's social security checks. He liked to work, to keep busy. Even while he was sitting and talking he left the impression that he would rather have been up and going. But narrating the falling bridge story had kept him glued to his chair.

"I didn't know that I was such a good runner," he said with a small smile. "I guess I was all of fifty years old at the time, too. It turned your blood cold to hear it falling. But I stayed ahead of it. It was a mess, boy, I'll tell you."

WILLIAM HELMS

He pronounced his name "Helums" and said that his father before him, and his father's father, were "Frank and Bill Helums" and that he "was borned in Terry Hote, and I come here when I was a lil baby."

We stood in the dazzling March sunlight outside a big, gray house at the end of a long private lane on Crooked Creek in Brown County. To shade his eyes, William "Bill" Helms, wore a corduroy billed cap that had seen better days. A faded plaid flannel shirt with a time-worn collar under a full denim jacket, Osh-Kosh B'Gosh bib overalls and ankle-top black shoes made up the remainder of his visible garb.

He was a short man and he smiled up at me. We'd been discussing the use of wood for heating the gray house, and as fuel for cooking fires.

"You git hot in the kitchen around a wood stove in the summer, sure," he said, nodding toward the house. "But we've allus been used t'that. Y'cain't change a man. When you take an ol' horse t'water y'cain't make him drink if'n he don't want to. Nope. You cain't change a feller. We allus cooked with wood and het with it."

A dyed-in-the-wool Hoosier, Bill Helms was perhaps the last of a vanishing breed. He at least was the kind of "feller" who could never be replaced. Since his arrival on Crooked Creek from Terre Haute he had enriched his immediate world with his being, his way of life, his manner of speaking, his simple honesty and his disarming congeniality.

"Oh, yes," he continued, "we burn wood the year 'round. I git them slabs from the Fleetwood Sawmill over near the tabernacle, you know. Wood heat's my best heat. Wouldn't give it fur no other kind, gas, nor fuel oil, nor nothin' like that."

Sawmill slabs were ricked at the far end of the neatly-kept yard, and there appeared to be enough to keep the gray house warm for a decade. As the late afternoon sun followed a golden path along the lane past us it reached the ricks and touched them gently, warmly. It stretched leisurely to caress the gray, tilting lean-to under which Bill's old pickup truck was parked, and the aged barn in which a mule named 'Jack' spent his nights.

"I keep a mule all the time," he said. "Use him t'drag out my wood and posts. Do anythin' I want with him. I've had several good ones in my time, and horses, too. But there ain't nobody much around here works them anymore. I work ol' Jack – he's fifteen – in the summertime pretty often. He works good. I had the harness on him last Friday. I drug out them posts down there with him. Keep him in the barn. Turn him out ever' mornin' and he takes off up there, yonder. I go get him of an evenin' and bring him back. That mule there, 'fore I ever bought him, I don't believe he ever seen a barn, or been inside one," he said.

A lone hawk patrolling the blue and white sky above us, the placidity of the old house in the long hollow, the steady chirping of birds, and the fugitive winter scents on the cold undulating spring wind set Bill Helms' world far from the one I had left only a few miles away.

"Aw, land no!" he exclaimed in answer to one question. "I worked at the univers'ty seventeen years, and when they was abuildin' that there Musical Arts Center them *bullnozers* and backhoes and other things was allus arunnin', and all those construction companies and the city and ever'thin'. Why, no, I wouldn't live in Bloomington if they give me the whole town. I'll tell you the truth, I wouldn't. I wouldn't live in no town."

As a child he walked a mile south of the house to join "fortee" other kids for studies in the one-room Crooked Creek School. He walked a mile back to his home in the afternoon. "These hollers in Brown County was just full of people then and they had big families," he said.

Across the road from the school house was the community church – the Crooked Creek Pentecostal Church. At the time of my visit with Bill, it was a lonely, vandalized, decaying structure. Bill remembered when it was the life of the lowland farming community of Crooked Creek.

"Aw, land yes!" he exclaimed. "People'd come from Bloomington and Bedford and Nashville t'church down here. Fur away? Not to people that wants to go t'church it ain't. Why you take 'fore cars got so plentiful, when they had church down here, they had revivals and the house was full. They came on horses and in buggies, 'n' everything."

He saw me look up at the martin house overhead on the tiny porch of which two sparrows sat. "Thought I'd get me a martin house and I'd have martins," he said. "Since then I've had bluebirds in it, and *spahrers*, and I've not seen a martin. They tell me it's too close t'the woods."

Bill lived in the gray house – the clean gray house – with his wife Lola. He pronounced her name *Lolie*.

He said she "belonged" to Silas Dewar before he met her. She was Silas Dewar's daughter. They had electricity and telephone service in the house, but water was packed from the back door yard.

"She's got a 'lectric washin' machine, but in the winter she does her wash mostly on a board, on account of it takes more water t'wash in the machine; more to pack. Lolie gets up at three o'clock in the mornin' to put water on t'wash with," he said.

Living in the country, "Eighteen miles east of Bloomington, 'n' three miles south of Nashville Road," early risings were a daily part of Bill and Lola's lives. For as long as he could remember, he had adhered to an eight o'clock bedtime. "No matter how much company we had, nor how long they wanted t'stay, we went t'bed at eight o'clock," he said. Wake up time was four o'clock. "I did my chores and then went on in t'work, and I never was *tardee* any mornin' on my job since I worked," he said proudly.

Two transistor radios provided Bill and Lola with news of their world. "We don't have a television," he said with a shake of his head. "That's somethin' I wouldn't give a dime fur. Tell you what, I'll just be honest with you. We got them two radios and we get news whenever. But as fur payin' from two t'five hundred dollars fur a television – I can take the money and put it in a bank and let it draw interest. And," he shook an admonishing finger at me, "there's what's the matter with this world t'day. All the young generation does is sits and watches television and that's why there's so much stealin' and *robberin'* goin' on. I say television is one of the worst things ever happened to the country. An' I ain't afraid t'tell you about it. And another thing," he held me with his clear blue eyes, "watchin' them things is hard on y'r eyes. Why, I wouldn't give y'a dime fur one. And radio's the same as television, only it don't have no picture. Lot of people won't watch a television without they see a picture. Why, that picture don't learn me anythin'. I ain't one t'run the other feller down, but I just don't want a television. And another thing. We're so low down in this holler a television, if we had one, wouldn't do no good. We'd probably have to put an *ay'ral* 'way up on that hill, so, therefore, I don't care nothin' about one," he said.

Storage areas in the big gray house abounded with the harvests of gardens past – all put up in jars. There were so many that Bill said he would have no garden that year. "I want to eat up what I've got," he said.

I asked him if he might one day leave the hollow; he had suffered a heart attack three years earlier, and he was nearing seventy. He surveyed the house, the twelve acres he owned that surround it, and he replied, "Ever'body says, well, y'been here so long if you'd buy out you'd never be satisfied. Which I don't know where I could go to be better satisfied than *ri'cheer*. It's nice and quiet here, 'n' cool in the summertime, and ever'thin'. I'll make out the best I can here, and just figure on stayin' here I guess."

He invited me to return, to "Come back and set awhile" and visit. I hoped that he would always remain in that hollow, that he would never change and, yes, that one day I would return. But I didn't.

THE KIMBRELS

When the insidious growths in his body finally overcame North Kimbrel at his home, they killed a man of strong faith. He had undergone a colostomy, had become critically ill with a suspected pneumonia that turned out to be cancer of the lung, and then developed cancer of the liver. At the time of his death, he had been fighting them for some months.

Because there were no daily press releases on his condition, no television specials about his life and its inexorable waning, you couldn't have known it. His was a simple passing. He died like most men die, quietly, practically unknown, and, as some men wish to do, he died at home.

During his automobile rides to and from the hospital for treatment as an out-patient, North would study the houses that went past the car windows. When he arrived at his own house near Owensburg, he'd invariably say to his wife, Ula, "This is the prettiest home of all." And he would add, "This is where I want to die – in our home."

The Kimbrel house was an unpretentious frame dwelling in the country. Clean and comfortable, it probably was just like yours, with the warmth of love and family its outstanding features. Also, like you and your family, North, Ula, and their children, all gave unselfishly of themselves to make that possible.

North was a churchman. Not all his life. Not that it should make a difference, for he was a good man even before he was baptized in The Kentucky Ridge Regular Baptist Church, near the Kimbrel home. One of his daughters, Barbara Book spoke of his goodness in this manner:

"There was always a lot of faith in our family. Dad was not a church-goer at first. He was always too busy trying to make a living. He worked all the time. And on Sunday, he'd rest. But he never drank, and he never smoked. He never even drank coffee. And he was always so good to us."

Ula took the children to church every Sunday. There were the girls, Barbara, her sisters, Phyllis Hagler and Judy Ward, and their brother David Lavon Kimbrel. And it was all right. When David emerged from a tragic affliction that deprived him of the sight of one eye, but miraculously left him alive with the strength to recover his health, North decided it was time to show his appreciation to God. He joined the church.

In the ensuing twenty-six years, he would become Sunday School superintendent and a church moderator. Believing himself unworthy to hold such an important position, he declined to serve as deacon. But he loved to sing, and he never passed up an opportunity to do so. His God had given him a voice, and he would use it in His name. He and Ula, and Beulah Gee, of Owensburg, sang at many services, many funerals. One day, toward the end of his life, North turned to Ula and said wistfully, "If I could get well, we'd go sing some more."

It wasn't to be. He would sing no more. His voice would never again be raised in song to the God whom he believed to be in a place called Heaven, a Heaven North believed was promised him, was awaiting him.

Though he was unable to sing again, he often, before his death, called praises to his God.

"The Lord has been good to us . . . The Lord won't put more on us than we can bear," he would repeat. Ula, a diabetic, had undergone a mastectomy and the surgical amputation of a leg. The Kimbrels were beset by expenses. Yet, in spite of this, he still raised his voice in praise.

Reiterating his belief in Divine assistance, North once told me, "The Lord has been good to us. We can tell you a thousand different ways He's been good to us. He's always had us something to eat. He's always given us a lot of friends. And we've always been a happy couple."

In an earlier column, I had detailed the circumstances surrounding Ula's mastectomy and the amputation of her left leg. "I was clipping my toenails and cut myself with the point of the scissors," she had revealed. "It was just a little thing on one of my toes."

The "little thing" soon became a gangrenous infection that required surgery. In a second surgery, her toes were amputated. In a third operation, she lost still another part of her left foot. A final effort to stem the spreading infection was made by amputating her left leg below the knee.

You've probably had similar calamities happen in your family. You've probably wondered why they all seem to happen in one place, and under one roof. And you've probably pounded your breast and shouted, "Why me?" Not North Kimbrel. His faith was unshakable. "The Lord," he would declare with conviction, "has been good to us."

North and Ula never had much as far as material things go. Yet, in thirty-six years of marriage they had achieved an enviable goal for poor folks, they didn't owe anyone. But medical and hospital bills had suddenly risen to frightening sums, and the Kimbrels found themselves with their backs to the wall. With North dying sick, and Ula with one leg, they could be of little help to each other. Still, North believed; he'd say with unshakable confidence, "The Lord will provide a way."

Readers of my column responded. Checks arrived in the mail. Canisters appeared in business places. Special collections were taken at churches. Contributions varied from hundreds of dollars, taken in a single collection at one church, to thirty-five cents from a little boy who had seen North's and Ula's names on a canister in a service station where he was poised, money in hand, before a soft drink vending machine. After inquiring about them, the youngster decided, "I don't need no soda," and dropped his money into the canister. When it was over, the Kimbrels had received enough money to pay their bills and to obtain an artificial limb for Ula. The power of the press? Perhaps. But North did not for a moment doubt that it was his Lord who had provided for them.

Ula also attributed her good fortune to the Lord. "I can't thank Him enough," she said. "The mailman brought something practically every day. It was such a shock. I was so overcome with gratitude I'd just have to sit and cry, and praise the Lord."

Ula had some problems with the new limb. In time, with the help of a cane, she learned to walk again. The fear that she had expressed after losing her leg – "You say to yourself, 'I wonder what I'll do if something should happen to my husband.' It's scary. It's an awful thing" – was alleviated.

One day, as North lay in the bed from which he would never rise, Ula, on her new leg, carefully made her way to his side and said with forced cheerfulness, "See my leg? Get out of there and let's dance." North laughed with humor and satisfaction. He had been worried about Ula's ability to care for herself. After witnessing her new self-confidence, he could rest in peace. His wife was capable of caring for herself. At last he felt ready to depart. His condition suddenly worsened.

"That's what he was waiting for," their daughter, Barbara said. "He was waiting to see that Mom could get along by herself. He was ready."

In just a few days, North summoned Ula to his bedside. "I want to go home," he told her softly.

"But you are home," Ula replied.

"No, I want to go to my home – " North held up a hand, reaching, it seemed, toward the ceiling " – up there."

"Of course," Ula said, "and soon we'll be up there together."

Those were the last earthly words North Kimbrel heard.

THE TOOLMAKER

There was an impish twinkle in his eyes when Elmer Bowman held out a strange looking cutter on a long wooden handle and asked, "What do you think this is?"

A circular blade some six inches in diameter was affixed onto the end of the wooden handle that reached from the ground almost to Mr. Bowman's wrinkled chin.

"A giant pizza-cutter?"

I was being facetious and suddenly I feared Mr. Bowman might not appreciate my kind of humor. But his wrinkled face broke into more wrinkles as he smiled and chortled, "That's what I told a feller. He said, 'What the heck is that?' And I told him, 'That's a giant pizza cutter.' You should have seen the look on his face."

The visitor's consternation was shortlived. Mr. Bowman confessed and told him the odd looking tool he was holding was a sweet potato vine cutter.

You'd have had to be in Mr. Bowman's company in the cluttered workshop behind his house in Freetown to have appreciated him and that strange garden tool. He'd made many useful things in that shop, including the sweet potato vine cutter.

Mr. Bowman – the b-o-w in his name is pronounced like the b-o-w in to take a bow, or the bow of a boat; seems everybody wanted to give it the sound of the b-o-w in bow and arrow – expressed pride in having not retired.

ELMER F. BOWMAN
The Toolmaker

"Oh, I get a Social Security check," he admitted. "But I work here all the time to keep myself going."

He did that by making tools, and by building dog houses, picnic tables, sawhorses, sawbucks, footstools, doll cradles, baby cradles, work benches and other wooden things.

"I don't make much money," he told me, "but I don't care as long as I can live and get by."

Getting by is never easy for most Social Security recipients. Fortunately for some, such as Mr. Bowman, who was eighty-eight when we met, they have found ways to supplement their doles. And would you believe that some people resent that?

"Somebody reported me," Mr. Bowman said. And after he was investigated, his monthly check was cut by thirteen dollars. He laughed. "Why," he said, "I couldn't make that much money if I worked at it."

Unless he had to go to town to keep an appointment, or perhaps visit the doctor, Mr. Bowman spent most of his time working in his shop.

"I went to the doctor last Wednesday," he said. "My daughter wanted me to. The nurse asked me a thousand and seven questions and then she let me see the doctor. 'How are you?' he said. I said, 'Fine.' He said, 'What are you doing over there at your place?' I said, 'I'm making dog houses, picnic tables, handles, foot stools, wood boxes and about anything else anybody wants.' He said, 'Well, you're in pretty good shape. Go on back and make some more.'"

Mr. Bowman gave me time to laugh and make a comment about that and then he said seriously, "But I can't see to make them all that good anymore."

To help him in that respect, he wore gold wire-rimmed glasses, the old fashioned variety with medium size lenses. The pads fit deeply into a long, aquiline nose shaded by a billed cap pushed down to the tops of his ears, one of which seemed pushed forward. Over a flannel shirt he wore a cardigan sweater and an ancient, patched overalls jacket over that.

Father of six, four of whom survived at this time, and grandfather to sixteen, and great-grandfather to twenty-six, Mr. Bowman had been widowed nineteen years. He had a brother who lived away from Freetown and a sister who lived nearby. He had outlived most of his friends, and although he smiled when he said, "I don't know anybody anymore," it made him sad. Still, when he learned the name of a visitor to his shop he could gratefully respond, "Oh, I sold a horse to your grandfather once," or, "Your husband's grandfather was my first school teacher," or, "Your grandfather and I did some logging together." And that's not so sad. In that manner, too, he could relate to the current community. And it helped that the town's kids called him "Uncle Elmer." That always brought a smile to his aged face.

Legally his name was Elmer F. Bowman. "Don't forget the 'F.' " he reminded me, "or I'll get the other fellow's duns. I got nine of them in twelve years once, and I had to prove who I was or I would have had to pay them. That was twenty-six years ago."

For a man his age, Mr. Bowman did some surprising things. For example, he had cut more than five-hundred ricks of firewood during the seven years prior to my arrival at his shop. A hundred and fifteen of them were cut on the same sawbuck, which got so grooved and notched in the process, it looked like it might have been overrun by legions of banqueting termites.

When my eye caught another strange looking tool and I asked its purpose, Mr. Bowman smiled and said, "That's the handiest thing on earth for what it's for."

He said he couldn't remember what he made it for. Whether he could or could not, or if he was attempting to pull my leg, I couldn't tell. But I did not insist on an answer.

TOMMY AND LYDIA

Tommy Baugh had gotten serious. He – or rather we – didn't begin that way. When Lydia, his wife, introduced us, he gave his head a shake and laughed. It was more a burst of laughter. And he was honest enough to say that it was precipitated by the sound of my last name. Lydia had pronounced it right all right. Perfectly so. Something few persons do when hearing it for the first time. But it struck Tommy funny, and he laughed heartily.

Then taking off what looked like a striped rain hat with the brim turned down, he shook his head again and said, "I couldn't say it if I knowed it." And he sat down across from me in the Baugh living room on North Russell Road, Bloomington. He'd been out of doors. Lydia said she'd have to call him. And while I waited inside, she stepped out of the back door and yoo-hooed to him a couple of times.

"He doesn't hear too well sometimes," she spoke to me back through the open door. "But I'll get him."

She did. She yoo-hooed him right into the house. When he was settled in his seat, and I said, "I'll speak up, so that you can hear me," Tommy held up a palm and drew in his chin. "Now," he cautioned, "not *too* loud."

I didn't speak too loudly. In fact, I spoke quite in a natural tone. Tommy heard every word, leaving me to wonder a few times during our visit why Lydia obviously believed her husband didn't hear too well. Toward the end of it – our visit – Tommy said something that could have been the reason for her believing that.

"We never did have a fight," he said. "There were a few times when we thought we were going to, but we didn't."

And Lydia had added, "That's right. When one of us starts talking too fast, the other walks away."

And I gathered from that, Tommy did a lot of walking away, which may have led Lydia to believe, despite his hearing aid, that he was hard of hearing.

They had reason to fight: They had been together for sixty-one years. Longer than that if you count the days they went to class together at Poplar Grove School, which was situated about a quarter mile south of Mt. Gilead Church.

But sixty-one years before I visited with them, Tommy and Lydia had traveled to the Mission Church on West Howe Street in Bloomington and were married by Rev. Joe Campbell. After the ceremony, they returned to Tommy's dad's house. They had no need of a honeymoon. Not even rings.

"We didn't believe in rings, and we don't want any," Lydia said.

Tommy was born on the place on Russell Road. It was a lot smaller than it was then, three-quarters of an acre from the one hundred sixty that were there when he was born. There were two houses on the land when I was at their home. Lydia was born about three miles from there, on another farm, on Bethel Lane.

Tommy made a scythe-like movement with his arm and said, "We've been right here all of our lives."

All of their active lives in that place Tommy farmed and Lydia was the wife of a farmer. Twenty-five of those years were given to the struggle of dairying.

"That's a dog's life," Tommy said in recollection of the hard work involved. "I mean it's every day. There's no let-up. You've got to milk twice a day every day."

"It was tough on the both of us," Lydia agreed.

It was one method of earning a living, Tommy admitted. He earned as little as a dollar sixty cents and as much as three dollars and fifty cents per hundred pounds of milk.

"That wasn't much money," he said. But he remembered an important consolation. "You could buy something with it."

"Yes," Lydia added, "You could buy a pound of coffee for twenty cents." Then she said, "And we killed our own meat."

For seventeen years of that long period, the Baughs operated a three hundred sixty acre farm in addition to being dairy farmers.

"Boy," Tommy shook his head. "You'd go and keep going as hard as you could go. And then you never got done."

I began this introduction to Tommy and Lydia by saying that Tommy had gotten serious. I somehow seem to have strayed, and have yet to tell you why he got serious. I'll do that now. It was the recollection of an accident he had while farming that brought on the mood. It lasted while he related it. And as he related it, I tried to see the eighty-one year old Tommy as a younger man on the verge of losing his life.

"The nearest to something taking my life," he began the account, "was when I got wound up in a combine, back in 1952. I stepped over the main shaft and a little bolt caught in my britches leg.

"It wrapped me up right now," he said. "But it killed the motor on the tractor. That was a miracle that would never happen again. As a rule, when there's a pull on the motor the governor opens up, and she takes off. But, this killed it.

"My son-in-law, Paul Anderson, was there. He took a knife and cut most of my clothes off to get me out. I was hurt bad, and I had to get to the doctor to have some places sewed up. It all happened so fast I didn't have time to get scared. It was quick as lightning," he said.

A smile suddenly broke through the solemnity of Tommy's countenance.

"Tell you what I did do that day," he said. "I came home in a sack. I had no clothes on from here down," he placed a hand at his waist. "So I cut the bottom out of a sack and wore it home."

Tommy had retired in 1962. Yet, he and Lydia remained active; caring for the place, gardening, and fishing had kept them busy. Tommy also had done a lot of coon hunting, but by this time he had given it up. They still loved to fish, and often did so at Lake Monroe – Paynetown or Moore's Creek, from the bank. Lydia would not get into a boat with Tommy. She said that Tommy shook it too much, and that she was afraid she'd get dunked, and she couldn't swim. She dunked herself accidentally about a year before when she was seventy-nine.

She and Tommy were fishing at a lake and she caught a little bluegill. In attempting to fasten the live basket to a stick in the bank, the stick, as she was pushing it into the mud, broke. Lydia plunged into the water head first.

"But I did swim," Lydia related what happened after she hit the water. "I went down twice. Then I swam. And I didn't do too bad, either.

"When I finally got back on the bank I looked awful. I had weeds in my hair. But I still had my teeth, my glasses and my shoes – and I went under twice, like I said."

At this point Tommy chortled. "You should have seen her go in. I saw her. She went in like a frog jumping in the water."

Lydia smiled and shook her head.

"If I could've got hold of him that day, I'd have pulled him in," she said. "He was afraid of me."

"She did scare me for a minute," Tommy said.

Life was not exactly dull after that experience. One day, as Lydia got up to leave church – the New Unionville Baptist Church where she and Tommy had been lifelong members – she tripped over the legs of a man sitting next to her, and she went sprawling.

Later, with bruised legs, she took the teasing of a granddaughter who admonished, "Granmaw, you should stay out of those wild places."

Sixty-one years is too often a lifetime, and for a man and a woman to share that many years in happiness is a blessing.

Tommy and Lydia agreed.

"It ain't been too bad," he said.

"There were a lot of things that made us happy," she said.

One of the benefits of this kind of bliss is that those who have it don't count the days – the years.

"I'd forgotten about our anniversary until one of the neighbors asked me what we had planned," Lydia said. "And now that we know that it is Sunday, we'll probably forget between now and then."

THE BAXTER PLACE

The trunk of the massive sycamore could have concealed a half-dozen kids playing "hide-and-go-seek," and the large limbs that reached out from it at right angles could have provided safe perches for a few dozen spectators. It was part of the attraction of the old house near which it rose into the sky, as were some poplars, elders, locusts, maples, and a pecan tree.

Lola Baxter had planted one of the maples some thirty years earlier – actually a maple seed, and at this time it was a giant tree. It had been twenty-five years since she and her husband, Aquilla, popularly known in the rural neighborhood as "Quill," had sent off for the pecan tree. It didn't bloom until the spring prior to my visit.

The outbuildings, too, added fascination to the old house; there were at least a dozen of them, including a huge barn. They were clustered in the bottomlands of Moores Creek Road, surrounded by high ridges on three sides, the fourth side opening out on Lake Monroe where the creek ultimately emptied into the larger body of water.

One of the ridges, which lay perhaps more north than any direction from the house, was called Snoddy. At one time children from the area went to school up there in a small building named Snoddy School, on Snoddy Road, which ran along Snoddy Ridge.

"They went until it closed down, and then they went to Handy School, and later to Sanders." Mrs. Baxter motioned almost carelessly toward another of the surrounding ridges. At least one of the Baxter children went to Snoddy School; they all went to Sanders.

The house was covered with long-unpainted clapboards, and it rose in three points, front and sides, to a story and a half. More than a hundred years old – Mrs. Baxter said at least a hundred and fifty – it originally was a two-room log house with the upper half-story making up a loft. The logs were still visible there, long, wide, hand-hewn sections, but they had been covered over on the lower floor. In the years after the original log section was built, additional rooms were attached until it became the house the Baxters lived in.

"Lots of people stop to look," Mrs. Baxter said of the old house's charm. "And an awful lot of them take pictures."

The house was known to old timers as "The Old Will Snoddy Place," and "Tick" is what they called Will Snoddy; Tick Snoddy. He died on one of the three inviting porches that were part of the attraction of the house. It happened on the south porch, after gangrene had set in a leg Tick had injured while working on the place.

Death very nearly visited the north porch one Saturday evening in 1958. Lightning struck the house just to the right of the kitchen door on that porch. It smashed the wall in, broke ten window panes, and burned out the electrical receptacles in two rooms. The Baxters, who were home at the time, were later told that had they been in either of those two rooms, they might have been killed. When they left the house to survey the damage to the wall next to the kitchen door, they also saw a spectacle for which they were unprepared.

"It looked like someone had built a big fire at the base of that sycamore," Mrs. Baxter pointed to a big tree. "And you could see where the lightning had hit one of the big limbs, and another limb was torn off and blown right over the house into the yard out front."

There was only one other time that the old house, or its surrounding ancient elegance was threatened by the elements. A sudden torrential rainfall had sent Moores Creek raging out of its banks, and its waters inundated the Baxter place. It rose in the barn, and the outbuildings, and they had to rescue some of their animals. Neighbor Jerry Pennington said he had never seen the creek do that in the sixty years he'd lived around there, and that was thirty years or more before my visit, Mrs. Baxter said.

A well on the north side of the house provided water for the Baxters. Another down by the barn supplied enough for their stock, then two cows and three calves. They had operated a dairy herd there once and had owned more than three hundred and fifty acres. They had since sold some, including about forty-four acres which became a part of the lake.

Mrs. Baxter washed clothes in a wringer washer, and on sunny summer days she hung them outside to dry. I had seen them flapping in the wind there a few times in what seemed a multi-colored semaphore emitting signals from a distant, glorious past. They had played a role in the overall charm that had drawn me to the old house.

"I hang them up on the top floor in the winter time," Mrs. Baxter said. "That's never been finished up there. In the summer it gets hot enough up there to roast eggs."

To complete the picture of the Baxter home on Moores Creek Road, Tippy, a twelve year old collie roamed the yard or basked in the many suns that had come into her life there.

"I wouldn't live in town if they give me a place there," Mrs. Baxter said. "There's plenty of wood here to burn to keep warm by."

There was an oil-drum heating stove Quill had made thirty-six years earlier to burn it in, too, and more than a few of the outbuildings seemed to bulge with firewood.

"Quill and his brother, Howard, cut ahead," Mrs. Baxter said of the abundant supply. "They say that if they get to where they can't cut, they'll be sure to have it around to burn."

Howard lived on one of the surrounding ridges, a sharp-backed one call Swartz Ridge. His home was known as the old Baxter place. He and Quill were the last of three brothers and three sisters born in the old house up there. It's a mile or more between the two houses, either down or up, depending on which way you're going, and Howard often walked it, with the up-walk usually coming after a day of cutting wood. At this time, he was either at his three-score and ten or past it.

Quill, like his wife, would never have settled for a place in town. But town was creeping closer to them. The spread of new homes, even then, seemed an ominous promise that one day town would reach out and overwhelm the charm of the Baxter place.

But for the rest of their lives, Quill and Lola Baxter remained "those lucky people" who owned and lived in that charming old house on Moores Creek Road.

HERLE'S

There seemed to be no one who remembered if, or when, it ever happened before, but for at least two days, in August 1974, the towering Greyhound buses passing through the small Orange County town of Orleans on their way south to Memphis and north to Detroit, did not stop.

Their drivers had decelerated perceptibly, though, especially as the imposing blue and white public carriers hummed past Herle's Cafe, the little restaurant with the sidewalk flag out front, on State Road 37.

"Maybe," ventured a native, "he's atellin' his passengers what all happened here."

Maybe. Maybe the drivers did announce to their passengers that for longer than they could remember Greyhound buses had been stopping daily at Herle's Cafe, the center-point rest stop between Memphis and Detroit. And maybe, if the passengers were interested enough to look out the deeply tinted windows, past the sidewalk flag, they saw the floral wreath and purple shroud fastened on Herle's locked door.

"Jess," the drivers might have continued, "JB Herle, the owner of Herle's Cafe and operator of the Greyhound agency here, the man who flies that flag every day, died on Monday. He was the town's oldest active business man."

HERLE'S CAFE
John B. "JB" Herle At Far Right, In the Mid-1930s

They might have spoken thus to their passengers while they paid homage to the deep purple crepe by slowing the big buses in a symbolic gesture of farewell to a beloved man and friend to many.

JB's body was even then being viewed at the Ochs Funeral Home. His widow, Edith; their daughters, Kathryn Waynick and Genevieve "Jenny" Hodson; Jenny's husband, Orville R. "Hoddy" Hodson; their families; and the loving school-age girls who waited tables at Herle's; they were all there.

They stroked JB's coat sleeve, the girls did, they tenderly caressed the stone-cold face, and being young and deeply hurt at the finality of death, they wept – hard, painful sobbings.

"They loved him," Kathryn said of the girls' affection for her eighty-two year old father. "They never passed his table but what they didn't stop to kiss him, or put their arms around him and ask him if he wanted anything, or just to touch him."

Since his arrival from his native Borden in 1915 and until his death, Jesse B. Herle flew the sidewalk flag every day. He was never away from Herle's, except at nighttime after the cafe had closed. During those years of devotion to the success of his restaurant-bus stop, his friends became legion, and among them were generations of youngsters who had waited tables for him.

A mother of teenagers herself, and one-time teenage waitress at Herle's, said of his passing, "The most loveable man in the world has died."

"He is," Orleans Chief of Police Dan H. Moffatt, insisting on using the present tense, said of JB, "one of the finest men I've ever known."

"Just always a gentleman, gracious and nice," remembered Mrs. Loral Grimes.

Wendy Opel, a twenty-five year veteran of the Indiana State Police Department remembered the many cups of coffee he'd drunk with JB.

"One of us managed to be in there at ten o'clock at night," he said of former troopers Paul Kern, Joe O'Brien, Jim Sutton, Wayne Marshall and Gene Cox. Ten o'clock was closing time at Herle's and the troopers were on hand to protect JB from someone who might take advantage of his kindness. "He was a father to all the kids at the time," Wendy said.

If anyone had taken advantage of his kindness, JB was never to reveal it.

During the years of World War II, as many as eighteen buses stopped daily at Herle's, giving the tiny small-town restaurant with the sidewalk flag out front nationwide notoriety. On second or third passings through Orleans, rest stops became reunions. Servicemen, befriended at Herle's, wrote letters of greeting and appreciation. Mail came from all over the U.S.

There was a mystique about Herle's when the big buses arrived and departed with their passengers, strangers from other places going to still other places. There was also the charm of native small-town congregations at breakfast time and the lunch hour with booths and tables ababble with local diners.

And there were always JB, quiet, smiling, friendly; Edith, pleasant, talkative, who in later life was called "Gran'maw" by almost all who knew her; and Kathryn and Jenny who grew up and worked in the small cafe, and Jenny's husband, Hoddy, who would spend more than four decades in the restaurant.

Suddenly JB was gone.

"He was just a good old landmark," mused Clarence Crowe, "and we're going to miss him."

Jesse and Edith had come a long way together. From April 13, 1913, when they were married, until JB's death, they had been man and wife for just a few moments short of 60 years. They had been in Orleans for so many years as owners and operators of Herle's Cafe it was said again and again that Orleans just wouldn't have been Orleans without them, their family, and their cafe.

"Where good friends meet," was Herle's business slogan which, in the course of pleasant times, became the personal invitation to countless thousands of travelers. Beginning with Blue Goose touring cars, Herle's was a rest stop for various commercial carriers. For a number of years it was under contract to Greyhound, the ultimate successor of those first carriers. Another, Fuqua Bus Lines, Inc., used to stop there on its runs between Owensboro, Kentucky, and Indianapolis, but not under contract.

Servicemen and draftees enroute by bus to stations around the U.S. during the war years were allowed seventy-five cents for a meal at Herle's. At the time of JB's death, GIs were allowed two dollars and twenty-cents. In their first year at Herle's, JB and Edith charged thirty-five cents for a plate lunch.

"We had a good time, and we enjoyed every minute," Edith said of their long career. For twenty-nine years they made their home in an apartment above the restaurant. Edith recalled those years this way: "It was down to work in the morning and up to bed at night. Never took a vacation until 1944."

JB was a quiet man. Edith, Jenny and Kathy by nature gave him little opportunity to speak. But he took his fate good-naturedly, spending his days in regal fashion totally content to sit and watch the activity in Herle's, accepting with a smile the pats, the hugs, the kisses his family and his employees bestowed on him.

He once told me that he attributed his longevity to "pretty girls, young girls," who through the years came to Herle's to wait tables and work in the kitchen. "They keep you young," he winked at me. "I just love him," Edith who was sitting beside him that day said, nudging him with an elbow.

After the Bank Holiday of the early 1930s had wiped them out financially, the Herles were aided on the road to recovery by the availability of a beer license. That was it, just beer. And until the 1940s when they gave up the beer license, Herle's was probably one of the few places in the state where people could sit side-by-side at a soda fountain and drink beer and milkshakes.

"The kids used to come over from Mitchell and Bedford and we'd push all the chairs to one side and dance," Edith recalled. "Oh, we had some good times. A lot of fun. They were all such fine kids."

Memories of having worked at Herle's after classes at the high school blossomed at the time of JB's death. One woman who worked there at an early age, returned thirty years later to work there three more times. She was Mrs. Deema Tolbert Compton. Mrs. Lillie "Honey Cup" Hunsucker spent more than forty years there.

The Herle's had come a long way, as restaurateurs, as man and wife, as father and mother to their daughters, as in-laws, and as grandparents and great-grandparents. The long way was fun, and funny, and easy, in so many ways. But there were a few thorns. Kathryn's husband, Ray, was killed in the crash of his plane during World War II; Jenny's and Hoddy's son, Barry, then nineteen, was struck on the head by a ball during a Sunday afternoon baseball game in the early 1950s and died instantly in view of the whole family; in February of 1978 Herle's was gutted by fire. It was rebuilt.

Edith, Kathryn, Jenny and Hoddy continued operating Herle's. It wasn't the same without JB. It would never be. Yet, it was still Herle's. Seven years after the loss of her husband, Edith died. The morning after her passing, Coleman "Pick" Pickens walked into Himebaugh's, a men's and boys' store then in Orleans.

"What time did Gran'maw die?" he asked, speaking the familiar nickname softly, almost reverently. His mood fit the ambience of downtown Orleans. That was about the way Coleman had walked into Himebaugh's, too, softly, almost reverently.

Pausing at the glass front door before pushing it slowly open, Pick had walked hesitantly, quietly to where Deema Compton stood behind the counter at the cash register. Everybody in small Orleans knew everybody else. Pick had known Deema for years. He also knew that Deema had worked at Herle's for many years and still worked there part-time, and that Deema and the Herles were all good friends, and that she would have the answer to his question.

"It was about five o'clock, Pick," Deema told him.

"Oh," he said softly. He nodded slightly, perhaps in gratitude of the information, but more than likely in sorrow at the finality of the message. And he left Himebaugh's.

At five o'clock the previous afternoon, Sunday, September 20, 1981, after a long and successful career as a wife, mother, mother-in-law, grandmother, great-grandmother, friend, and small town restaurateur, Edith Herle had gone to her reward.

Five hours before her death, the small cafe had served more than two hundred fried chicken dinners at its Sunday noon meal.

"Through the years, this place has made many friends," said Kathryn. "And very often people have gone out of their way to return to say hello to Mother. They called her Gran'maw. It didn't matter if they were young or old, everybody called her Gran'maw."

"Her life was her customers," Jenny said. "She lived to see them every day, and when she couldn't be in here, she'd be put-out, unhappy. She was happiest when she was making friends."

Edith would pitch in to help Kathryn and Jenny, and Jenny's husband, Hoddy. But usually she would sit in a booth or at a table, satisfied to hold court with those attracted to her small-town sociability. Sometimes she would complain of her ills, but only because they limited her activity. She was never without the will and the desire to do.

"Even during this last illness she was put-out because she couldn't be here helping," Kathryn said.

"She was quite a person," Jenny added.

After Pick had walked slowly through the glass front door of Himebaugh's and into the sunshine, the telephone in the store rang.

"I don't know yet," Deema spoke into the mouthpiece. "We'll just have to let you know."

"The women from the church," she spoke to two other ladies in the store, Irma Williams and co-owner of the store Eleanor Himebaugh. "About the food. They want to know how much they should fix, and when."

The women looked at one another. Deema remembered her many years at Herle's and that she still worked extra there on Sundays. Irma had been a waitress there in the 1930s. The women thought about the dozens of women and girls who down the years had worked at Herle's. They would have to be considered with Edith's many other friends and restaurant customers who would also attend the funeral service.

"There are so many they'll have to fix for," Deema said. "Gran'maw was well liked. When folks came to Herle's they generally came to see her."

Outside Himebaugh's a Greyhound Scenicruiser filled the day with a shushing of its air brakes as it reduced speed. It had happened again. The driver had seen the shrouded wreath on the cafe's front door. In a moment the bus picked up speed and was gone.

In August of 1988 Hoddy died at age eighty-five. He and Jenny had been married fifty-four years. Hoddy had spent more than half his life in Herle's and had won countless friends and the respect of the entire community.

A native of Milan, he taught school at Cambridge City, Rising Sun, Campbellsburg, West Washington, Hardinsburg and Orleans public schools. He coached basketball, baseball, track and other sports at all of them. After hours he coached American Legion and independent baseball teams, and in his last exhausting days, he coached youngsters from a swing in the park.

At the time of his death, Hoddy's beneficiaries were in great abundance. In commemoration of what he gave to so many, the practice field in the town park was named in his honor. He had given more. He was coaching first base in 1955 when his son was felled by a baseball. Hoddy was devastated, so heartsick his hair turned white overnight. But in spite of some criticism, he continued to encourage young people to participate in competitive sports, and he continued to coach them.

During his early years at Orleans High School, one of his students was Jenny Herle. She set her hat for him and they were married after she graduated. Her diploma bore his signature.

After JB's death, Hoddy continued to fly the sidewalk flag in front of Herle's. "He was insistent about that flag being out there," Jenny said. He was even more insistent than JB that the flag was in place every day. On June 14, Flag Day, 1986, the year before he died, Hoddy was honored for his patriotism when The National Society of the Daughters of the American Revolution presented Herle's with a plaque in recognition of the daily display of the sidewalk flag.

Its presence was not without incident. Three times it sustained damage of one kind or another. None was so bad as when a leviathan Greyhound bus was accidentally backed into it. Each time it was repaired and replaced, to again fly there in the same spot.

In 1989 Jenny's and Hoddy's daughter, Linda, and her husband, Bob Harris, were the new owners of Herle's. When Bob became ill sometime later, the couple had to give up the restaurant. A memorable era had come to an end.

Through the years Herle's had become a favorite interlude for me. On my way to or from a story in the area of the small cafe, I made it a point to stop there. It was always like coming home. The Herles, the friendly townspeople who frequented the place, the waitresses, good home-cooked food, and pies. It was very special.

The victim of time, the Herle's we all knew is no longer there. I miss it. I remember I was that impressed with it after my first visit many years ago that I wrote these prophetic words:

"It was a new experience, this stop at Herle's," I wrote. "And it was difficult, painful to terminate – like maybe none of it will ever be there again. I knew, then, that the only sadness at Herle's was in departing . . . "

BRIDGE TO ANOTHER TIME

Rains had swelled Hunter Creek, but not quite like they had when Granpaw Bill Todd died and his funeral had to be delayed until his body could be safely taken to Gilgal Cemetery for burial.

The small tributary was known to react to heavy rains that way. It winds south through northeastern Lawrence County to join Henderson Creek and together they move on to make the Little Salt.

One time, Cleta Murphy remembered, as did her husband Berlin, the overflow covered fields from hill to hill east of the creek bed.

Still, on this particular Saturday, the water was up and rushing, and there was an undercurrent of foreboding about it while Uncle Logan Todd, who had ridden down on horseback, and Elza Robbins, who had come in his wagon, waited in the roadway.

"We were going to Granmaw Derotha Todd's," Cleta said. "We lived in Smithville and Dad had brought us this far in his old open-top Chevy. The water was up high and Elza was aiming to take us across in the wagon and Uncle Logan was going to help.

"Beth was the baby then," she marked the date in typical rural Hoosier fashion, "and there were Ray, Wilma, Marie, Lena, Reatha, Marion and me. Eight of us, and Mom and Dad. We were all loaded into Elza's wagon. When he started the team across the

Bridge at Hunter Creek

water, one horse balked. It got a leg across the wagon tongue and went down in the water. The current caught the wagon but luckily washed it back to the bank. Dad stood up then and handed us out one at a time to Uncle Logan who was waiting there.

"Just after we all got out safely, the wagon, with Elza still in it, turned over and went under. I can remember Elza coming up and grabbing his hat. They found the horses later; they were all right. But they never did find all the pieces of the wagon."

Years later, when Marie was sixteen, Everett Blackwell bought the old Cleve Clark house on the east bank of Hunter Creek and moved his wife Dertha and their large family from Smithville to it. He also moved a large red barn from Hickory Grove Ridge to that property, and it still stands.

"And the year Dana Joyce was born was the year we either built this house, or we got electricity that year," Cleta said uncertainly.

The house is of red brick tile and as travelers pass along State Road 446, it beckons invitingly, warmly from the base of a hill that rises sharply at its back.

From the comfort of a chair on the brick-railed porch across the front of the house, where a cool breeze finds its way to him from the uncomfortably hot and humid world without, a visitor can view the old roadway, Hunter Creek, the adjacent cornfields and the newer highway beyond.

"When we used to come here to visit Granmaw Todd, the only road was between the creek and where the new road is now," Cleta said. "To get to the road from here you had to ford the creek; there was no bridge."

Sometime during the Depression, federal dollars were allocated to relocate the road so that it passed directly in front of the red brick tile house that

Everett Blackwell built, and to erect a bridge over Hunter Creek; an iron suspension bridge, it is not an uncommon structure. Long plank runners rising like inverted ruts at right angles to its thick wood floor, and rust-coated side supports and rails, it is prosaically agrarian southern Indiana.

Blackwell children used to play in the creek in the shadow of the bridge and rode their horses bareback over it on their way to and from services at Hunter Creek, Blackwell and Hickory Grove Pentecostal churches.

"Lena and I were the field hands," Cleta smiled. "We plowed and cultivated with horses. One of us would drive and the other would handle the plow or the cultivator. It didn't matter then if you were a boy or a girl, we were the oldest children so we did what had to be done. When the boys got big enough to work, they had tractors."

Near the end of World War II, Everett and Dertha Blackwell were listening to the radio and heard a report that American troops were entering Germany. Everett interpreted the announcement as a message of ill omen.

"Here's where we lose our boy," he predicted to Dertha.

Soon after that, the Blackwells received a telegram from the War Department informing them that their soldier son, Marion, had been killed in action.

Death also came to Granmaw Todd and Uncle Logan Todd. Before long, Dertha passed on. Everett died just short of his ninetieth birthday.

The days of innocence at the red brick tile house on Hunter Creek were over. But the good days live on in the recollections of those who remember them. Anyone who lived in the vicinity and was going any place, had to pass there when they crossed the bridge. That changed when in later years, the new road was built beyond the cornfields and far to the west of the Blackwell house.

After that only those few families that lived on the old road, the rural mail carrier, the newspaper motor route person, a few hunters, and those drawn to the place because of its aesthetic surroundings drove past the red brick tile house and across the old iron bridge.

When the bridge was closed to traffic in later years, until it could be repaired, no one passed there. The house was eventually sold to Everett and Dertha's son, Ray. While he was waiting to take possession, Cleta and her husband, Berlin, spent part of their fiftieth year of marriage there.

THE EUCHRE PLAYER

Lavon "Buck" Byers so enjoyed the card game of euchre, he walked a mile and a quarter every day to play it with friends. Not far, you say? Maybe not for you. But for Buck, who was eighty-seven at the time, it was quite a jaunt. He not only walked the distance to play the game, he also walked the distance when he retraced his way home at the end of the day.

Buck lived at 1255 S. Seminary St., in Bloomfield. His son, Franklin, lived nearby at 1308 S. Seminary St. Franklin put a stop to Buck's daily hikes. He felt that a mile and a quarter each way was a bit much for a man his father's age, especially in cold weather. So he began giving him a lift in his car.

Buck played euchre every day at the Senior Citizen Center on W. Main St. Like so many other elderly, Buck was up early and ready to go when most of us were still asleep. And Franklin had to be ready to chauffeur his father, or Buck, who never tarried, would set out on foot and leave him behind.

"He thinks," Franklin said with a laugh, "that he's got to be there before daylight."

Not exactly. Buck just liked to be at the center early. He liked being there to greet the first arrivals of an average of a couple dozen daily visitors to the place. Except for a brief break at noon for lunch, he would be there all day. Some days, if there were enough warm bodies on hand to have "another" game, and they could have supper brought in, Buck would stay late. In either case, when the day was over he'd hike the mile and a quarter home to bed.

Buck did this six days a week. On the seventh day he'd ride to the service at the Antioch Christian Church with Franklin and his wife, Mary Alice. Buck's wife, Ines, had passed on ten years earlier and was buried there in the church cemetery. Her death was the worst thing to ever happen to Buck.

She was Ines Foster, from around Mineral City, when they met at their jobs at the old furniture factory in Bloomfield. Buck lived in Switz City at the time, one of sixteen children reared in two marriages by his father. That's where he learned to play the game of euchre.

"I was that high," Buck held a hand palm down at knee-height. "My father used to say, 'I'd rather my children would play euchre here at home and I know where they're at.' "

Not many people felt that way about cards in those early days.

Buck and Ines had five children. Franklin, Wilma Emery, and Oleta Long of Bloomfield; Mildred Childers of near Shelbyville; and Betty Pearson of Bloomington. After the death of his parents, Buck's nephew, Frederick Alexander, also became a member of the family.

"I treated them all the same," Buck said of the six children who lived under his roof. "And," he added proudly, "I put all six of them through high school."

That was a feat, considering that Buck never earned more than a dollar and sixty-five cents an hour in more than fifty years at the furniture factory.

"But," he hurried to point out, "we raised our living on the farm. We had our milk and eggs, butter and meat. And we were able to save some. Times," his voice took on additional sincerity, "weren't too tough, and they weren't too easy. But I'd say we lived better on a dollar and sixty-five cents an hour then than folks do now on five dollars an hour."

Early in life, Buck got into the habit of retiring early and rising early. Although he was retired, he continued the practice.

"I get my best rest in the fore part of the evening," he said. "I'm generally in bed by eight or eight-thirty. And I'm up at four. I've got the first light that's turned on in the morning in the neighborhood. I'll toss five or six slices of bacon and a couple of eggs in the skillet, eat it all with bread and water (Buck never drank anything else), make up my bed, take a bath, read a while, and then come here to the center."

When Franklin rose at five o'clock, he would look out to see if his father's light was on.

"He wants to live by himself," Franklin said. "He does. But I always check for that light. When I see it, I know that he is all right."

Buck smiled about that and the loving concern all his children had for him.

"Their mother was the boss when she was living, and the kids all went to bossing me when she passed away," Buck said with a smile. "They'll growl at me a lot. 'Now Dad, don't do this, don't do that, don't do the other,' " he mocked their concern for him.

"I don't mind," his smile broadened until he burst out laughing. "I listen, then I go on and do as I please," he said between guffaws.

Buck's children also "growled" at him at Christmastime, he said, when he presented them with forty-four gifts for them, their children, and their children's children.

Still laughing, Buck said, "But I tell them, 'If I give it to you now, you won't have to fight over it when I die.' And I also tell them that I won't have to pay taxes on it if I live."

If Buck comes across as a pretty nice guy, take my word for it, he was.

"He's just always been a peaceful guy," said Franklin. "He was a good neighbor to help anyone, and he always worked hard all his life. He was always a good father, always good natured, and he took time to help us when we were in trouble. And he always saw to it that we had those things we ought to have had. He put us all through high school, too. And he put our cousin through high school, just like he did us."

Until the government took it away from him a few years earlier, Buck was one of the few remaining World War I veterans receiving a monthly pension. When we visited, he subsisted on a Social Security stipend and a small pension from Crane Naval Ammunition Depot where he worked after the furniture factory shut down. He retired from Crane at age seventy-four.

So his retirement days were spent playing euchre with friends. He enjoyed it so, he was willing to walk a mile and a quarter each way just to be with them.

THE GOLDEN SPUR

With the price of gold as high as it is, this would be an ideal time to uncover the "golden spur." Do you have it? Maybe in a junk pile in the attic . . . the garage . . . shed? It was purchased at a public auction several years ago, and it is believed the purchaser had no idea of what he or she was buying, and now may have. Let me relate the story of that spur as it was told to me by John W. West, who lived on Sassafras Road, Linton.

West, who was seventy-eight when he told me this story, said he saw the golden spur in the 1930s. He hefted it, he said, and he guessed it weighed a pound and a half – a small fortune in gold today. And West, his wife, Dorothy, and their young son, Jim, stood there and watched the owner whittle on it, like it was a piece of wood. Jim, who was fifty when I visited with his father, remembered that he figured "About six dollars in gold shavings fell to the floor." But let me tell you this strange story from its beginning, as West began it.

"My oldest boy," he said, after I had drawn up a chair, "had a kidney ailment. The doctor told me that the best thing I could do was to get him into Riley Children's Hospital, in Indianapolis. Then he said, 'I'm going to tell you, and I want you to go home and tell your wife, that boy'll never grow up.'

"Well," West continued, "that boy was in and out of Riley Hospital for nine years. We'd take him there by car – me and my wife. She died in 1961. And usually we'd drive up there and back on a Saturday. Well, we were coming back home this one Saturday, and near the little village of Carp, there in Owen County, we – me, my wife and Jim – stopped and picked up this old fellow who said he was going to Spencer. He said he was going there to visit his boy.

"Now I'm a collector of Indian rocks," West spoke softly, somewhat hesitantly. "Not much. But some. And this old fellow said he had some Indian rocks. Anyway, on another Saturday coming back from Indianapolis, we – me, my wife, and Jim – picked him up again. And he told us that he'd found another awful good relic, and that we should stop in at his home, there in Carp, to see it.

"We didn't that day," West said. "But on one of those trips back we did. That old fellow told us he was eighty-four years old, and that his wife was eighty-two. He said they didn't have a lick of medicine in the house 'cause they didn't need any, and that they'd never been to a doctor or a dentist, and that they were both in the best of health. Anyway, we looked at his Indian rocks. He had a few nice ones. Then he brought out this big spur. And here's the story he told about it.

"He said that as a boy he lived down around Salem, down in southern Indiana. One day, he said, they got word that Morgan and his raiders were in Salem. And the men all around the neighborhood saddled up their horses and took their guns and rode off for Salem, to fight him off."

(Early in July of 1863, Confederate General John Hunt Morgan and his raiders had approached Vernon, Corydon, Paoli, Palmyra, Versailles and other southern Indiana towns. A number of them were reportedly captured by them. It was reported that during his raids the small town of Gosport had armed itself against Morgan and his band. A rumor that Morgan was near a town sent armed men on horseback to fight him off. Thus it was at Salem.)

"Well," West continued, "he told me that after the men rode off from his place, he was standing in the yard and he saw five or six men riding up on horseback. There was an open well on the place, one with a pulley, and a bucket at the end of a rope. And there was a gourd hanging there for a dipper.

"Well, those men stopped at the well, and one of them pulled up some water and filled the gourd. And he said, 'Come here, boy.' He wasn't mean, or anything like that. And when he was close enough, the man made the boy drink out of the gourd. He wanted to see if the water in the well was poisoned, you see. When he was satisfied that it wasn't, all the men drank, and they watered the horses.

"This old fellow told me that there were several canteens laying around that the horsemen were going to fill with water, you see. But for awhile they just sat around talking. And one of them took off a spur and went to working on it. The rivet that held the rowel was broken.

"It wasn't but just a little while," West said he was told, "and there was some shooting on the other side of a hill. Those men jumped up and mounted their horses and rode off. They left behind their canteens and the spur that rider had been working on. The old fellow told me that he picked up the spur and carried it into the house, and that he'd had it ever since.

"Now, then, some years later when he was a grown man, he was down in the south – Kentucky or Tennessee, I don't remember now – and he heard that

Morgan's Raiders were having a reunion. (Morgan was not present. He was killed by Union soldiers in September, 1864.)

"By this time he'd pretty well figured those horsemen at his house when he was a boy were Morgan's men, the old fellow said. So he went to that reunion. And he was talking to some of them and he said, 'I've got one of you fellow's spur.' And he told about that day at the well at his home near Salem.

"Well," West went on slowly. "He said an older man there walked over and put his hand on his shoulder and said, 'Young man, you've got John Morgan's spur.' And he said that man said, 'You go home and count the teeth in the rowel. If there're thirteen, then that's John Morgan's spur.' And then he said the man told him, 'It's solid gold.' He said he came home and counted the teeth in the rowel, and that there were thirteen," West recounted the old fellow's story.

"It didn't look like real gold," West recalled his, his wife's and his young son Jim's impression of the spur. "It was a dark color. Some of the teeth on the rowel appeared to be broken. And there was some damage where the rivet holds the rowel. But to show us that it was really gold he went to whittling on it with a knife.

"Not long before that President Roosevelt had called in all the gold in the country, and people were being paid thirty-three dollars an ounce for it. So I asked the old fellow, 'Do you know what that thing is worth?' He said he wasn't interested in money. He said he wouldn't part with that spur."

West identified the old fellow who told him this story as Morris Crowe. He believed he was a brother to country violinist Walter Crowe, who used to entertain in county schools when West himself was a boy. Morris Crowe had a son, in Spencer, named Montgomery.

Both are deceased. Their worldly possessions, through the mechanics of estate settlements, were scattered at public sale.

Among those possessions was General John Hunt Morgan's golden spur. Do you have it? Maybe in a junk-pile in the attic . . . the garage . . . shed?

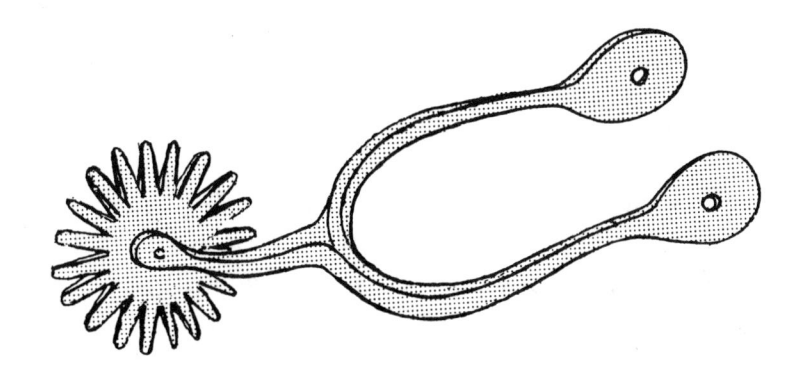

KELLY REED

It was coincidence that the building at the end of the mile-long, green leafy-tunnelled driveway should be a log house two stories high with white mortar between the hewn dark brown surfaces of the logs. At first appearance coming up the long, long driveway the structure seemed to jump out of the pages of a history book of early America; isolated in a green clearing, sturdy, quiet, fortlike.

Then, too, there were dogs – four of various ancestries who answered to the names Captain, Rags, Blue Boy and Blackie. Their barking rent the tranquility of the place and their white teeth flashed threateningly until they were calmed by the raspy voice of Kelly Reed.

Kelly Reed, one-time vaudevillian, bell hop, hotel manager, banker, had purchased the one-hundred sixty acres in the mid-Twenties. In his past at that time were a childhood in Mt. Vernon in Posey County, later months of hitch-hiking around the U.S.A., and service during World War I aboard the U.S.S. Georgia and the U.S.S. Chin Chow, an old bucket he said should have been scuttled before the inauguration of Teddy Roosevelt.

In 1933, after three years of manual labor by himself and his brother, the log house was completed. Five huge fireplaces heated its ten or a dozen rooms (a visitor easily lost count) which were decorated with a lifetime of memories.

"I came back from the war with eighty dollars in the pockets of my hundred and thirty dollar suit," Reed reminisced aloud in his raspy voice. The rasp was the result of an accident. A friend many years ago was demonstrating a Judo chop to the Adam's apple and failed to stop it in time. "It almost killed me," Reed smiled, "but I lived through it and wound up with this," and he placed a hand at his throat, about as near as he could come to placing it on his voice.

The hundred thirty dollar suit would last, but the eighty dollars in cash would not. But Reed was born under a strangely lucky star.

"I was always a very fine ballroom dancer," he recalled, "and one night a friend suggested I go on stage."

Reed teamed up with Helen Jelf, a name few of today's theater-goers will recognize, and he made his debut in Chicago. He earned a fabulous salary of seventy-five dollars a week and the stage was his life for five years.

"They were good years," Reed said of his theater life, "and if it hadn't been for this," and again he raised his hand to his throat, "I would have stayed with it."

Those were the years new faces were appearing on stage – unknowns such as Bob Hope, Jack Benny, John Charles Thomas, Lili Pons, Earl Carrol, Wally Ford, Myles Pebble and a host of others. Reed knew all of them and they were all to meet again, along with John and Ethel Barrymore, after Reed became a well-known and respected figure in the hey-day of Chicago's plush hotels.

"During those years on stage I was offered an opportunity to dance on tour which would have taken me, among other places, to China. But my mother was too sick to travel and I turned it down," Reed remembered.

His mother spent her years in the log house after it was completed and it was here, too, that Reed spent his vacations and every free moment he could beg or borrow. It was a refuge not only for him, and at times for his three brothers and two sisters, but also for many of show business's famous names.

"This has always been such a lovely place," Reed said of the log house and surrounding acreage. The structure was situated a mile off Clay Lick Road in northeastern Brown County, where Reed's closest neighbors were the trees, the birds and the wild animals.

Among the names of past years that came from Reed's reminiscing were mixtures of the unknowns and the famous, and that's the way they came out of his mouth, too. "Audrey Gibson and her sister, Eva," he said, and then in the same breath, "Lindy, Queen Marie of Rumania, Marion Kingston and Sir Aubrey Smith."

A man can stack up a lot of memories in seventy-five years and, if they come from his storeroom in the disorder of their occurrences, they make for more interesting listening. Like when Reed went from Queen Marie and their meeting in Chicago in the Twenties to boxing Andy Ward and Ray Jog in the Navy during World War I. And, long before that, taking lessons to become a jockey from the famous Phil Muskgraves of that day. Lessons which came to an end when Muskgraves was thrown from a horse in a race in Maryland and killed.

The interior of Reed's log house was itself like something from the stage or screen. The main living room was surrounded by a balcony onto which a number of bedrooms opened. Two other sitting rooms were included on the main floor and another was on the second floor. Every room was done in the decor of a different time and antiques abounded in each.

Most impressive of those pieces was a cathedral bench from Italy which stood more than nine-feet high and was six-feet wide.

"It has been appraised at fifty thousand dollars," Reed said. "But I'd sell it for fifteen thousand."

Amy F. Bell Reed came to live in the log house in the Thirties and never left the place. She died at eighty-four on December 12, 1950. Ten years before Reed and I met, Norman D. Phillips, a furniture upholsterer, came to live with Reed and was still with him. Phillips had a work shop on both the first and second floors of the building.

"We love this place," Reed said as his pale blue eyes scanned the surrounding woodlands from which he had cut and dragged trees to the site of the log house. A breeze moved easily through his straight, gray hair which an early photograph revealed was once black and wavy. "We love it," he repeated. "There are many memories here, good ones. Sad ones, too. But mostly good. There just isn't another place like it in the whole world."

After a pause and a puff on a Pall Mall he added, "We are going to add another room on to the house. We need the space."

I took his word for it.

BLANCHE TRACY

A vintage Hoosier reared and seasoned in the pitcher-pump, coal oil lamp and wood stove era, Blanche Tracy had something in common with each of us. A delightful lady who sold books, magazines and newspapers in Nashville, she believed her life would make an interesting book. But between memory and accounting, there was an obstacle.

"It's up here," Blanche touched a delicate finger to the thinning silvery sheen that covered her temple. "Only I can't seem to get it out to put it down on paper."

Pausing briefly to shake her head and pull back her lips in what was meant to be a gesture of helplessness, she added: "I look at the Foxfire books and I think, 'I've lived through a lot of that.'"

Blanche lived through more. As a matter of fact, since the years of the pitcher-pump, Blanche often felt that she had lived two lives – that she had been two persons, neither of whom was capable of writing her life story.

Blanche was born in 1896, the last leap year before the turn of the century and claimed to be an eighty-three year old lady who had celebrated only nineteen birthdays. She didn't kid herself about her years, however. When an acquaintance returned to Nashville after an absence of several months and said in greeting, "I was afraid to come by; I was

Blanche Tracy

afraid you'd gone to Heaven," Blanche's eyes sparkled and she smiled slyly, "Not yet," she said.

"I don't try to fool myself," her smile was suddenly wistful. "I know more people buried in the Unity Baptist Church cemetery than I know anywhere else. There was a time when I'd tell the kids when I felt bad that I'd be all right in a day or two. I know better than to say something like that now. Life's a day to day thing now. There are no more big decisions. But," her words quickened, "I don't like to dwell on sad things. It's been fun to live and I appreciate life deeply."

Daughter of Irishman John W. Murphy and his wife, Olive Gordon, Blanche was reared on a farm north of Nashville, between what then was called "The Big Road" (now State Road 135), and the village of Unity, at a time when families were a wealth unto themselves.

"We all grew up as one big family in that area," she recalled, "There was hardly a home that didn't have a grandparent or an uncle or somebody who was being cared for in it. We didn't mind," she hurried to say. "It was expected. We were crowded, of course, but we had a warm, stable family life."

Forty-eight years before we met, after her husband James Everett Tracy set up a sawmill on a Nashville lot and cut and built the eight room Tracy home in which Blanche still lived, that warmth and stability continued; the Tracy's had six children, four daughters and two sons.

"And," Blanche said, "we always had somebody in the house living with us. It was a good life. It was a rich life; so good and so rich that there is so much to say for it that if I got started talking about it good, I wouldn't know where to stop."

Her life was not confined to the house with its family and its other occupants. While Everett was the county treasurer, Blanche served as his deputy. In later years, as a widow, she would win a primary and an election to become the county's first female treasurer.

Public life also included twenty-four years as a clerk in Bonnie Fleetwood's General Store. After Bonnie's death in 1968, Blanche spent six months closing out the store for Bonnie's husband, Herbert.

"If you couldn't find it any place else, you went to Bonnie's," Blanche said during a fond look back at the old general store.

She was also employed by Portia Sperry, in what became the Brown County Folks Shop, in the Nashville House. For nine years prior to our meeting, she had been working in Nashville's Book Nook.

"I can say in all honesty," she said in reviewing her public life, "that in all the places that I've worked, I've never had an unpleasant experience."

She was not so fortunate in her private life; a son, Jim was fatally injured twenty-seven years earlier in a traffic accident at the Belmont Bridge; ten years after that she lost her husband; and she had witnessed the burials in the Unity Baptist Church cemetery of members of six generations of the Murphy family.

"We lived and we died," she said musingly. Brightening she added, "But we've always had a laughable side to us."

Blanche explained why she counted only nineteen leap year birthdays.

"A lot of people find it hard to understand," she said. "At the turn of a century there was a lapse of eight years instead of the usual leap year four. So you see, I was eight years old before I had my first birthday. And I had my picture in the *Indianapolis Star* when I had it."

Blanche had found immeasurable pleasure in work, which remained an important role in her life.

"I don't need it," she said. "But I do like to keep in touch with people. And work is a pleasure. It is an enjoyable thing to do; it is an enjoyable thing to be able to do it."

She was the last person who would try to sell someone on the fallacy that life is a bowl of cherries.

"But," she pointed out, "if you lose your temper – and leave it lost – and if you force yourself to learn to adjust, and to fake it, life can be more pleasant. You may not be happy, but you'll be satisfied."

An aid to that end for Blanche was religion; religions.

"I've taken from the different churches a lot of what I like best about them," she said. "And I've come up with a pretty sound foundation for happiness and satisfaction."

The pitcher-pump era was remembered by Blanche as a good time to have lived.

"We never worried about utilities like we do now," she said. "The pitcher-pump was always available, a gallon of coal-oil cost a dime, and wood was for the cutting. If you went cold, it was because you were lazy.

"We were independent and without fear," she continued. "If we had seventy-five dollars in the fall, and our taxes were paid, we wintered good. It was such a good life.

"Today," sorrow crept into her voice, "you go up and down the street with fifty dollars to pay your utilities and it's like having nothing. And when the lights go out you feel pretty helpless.

"I feel sorry for the young people," she said. "I worry about how they're going to make it through this."

GRANDPAW'S TREASURES

A neighbor smiled and said that Floyd Stahl's front porch in Arney "looks like the awfullest pile of junk that God ever made," but, just before that, a little girl from Sydney, Australia, took one look and she said, "That's Grandpaw's treasures."

Floyd, a smiling, bright-eyed man, simply said, "Well, now, what do you think? I bought an old ice box for two dollars and I sold it for a hundred."

The enormous collection on the Stahl front porch was only a fraction of Floyd's treasures. Some were in the yard around the house, which was situated a few miles from Freedom on the Freedom-Coal City Road. Additional untold amounts were jammed from back to front in several outbuildings. By the time it was to be completed, still more of Floyd's treasures were to fill another outbuilding, then under construction.

"Mister," Floyd said, pulling back the corners of his mouth and shaking his head and moving a hand in a sweeping gesture that would have included the entire Stahl yard and outbuildings had we been outside, "you don't have any idea; there's a lot of things out there."

As massive as his collection was, he nevertheless managed to keep an inventory of it – in his head. And, at that moment, he was aware that an old tea kettle and several items were missing, probably stolen.

Floyd became interested in cast-offs early in life, when he once attempted auctioneering. "But, we had two children and I couldn't make a living at it," he said.

It wasn't until 1967, when his wife became ill and he quit a construction job to be with her, that he began collecting seriously. "I went to farm sales, and I traveled a radius of fifty-sixty miles around," he said.

At sixty-nine, and alone since the death of his wife, he still attended farm sales. And he still traveled a radius of fifty-sixty miles buying and collecting treasures. His efforts won him a widespread sale of items, not to mention a satisfactory living.

"I've got horseshoes in Texas, an old telephone in California, a sled and sausage mill in New Hampshire, a grindstone in Georgia, and an ice box in Minnesota. I've got things sold all over," he said.

Floyd attributed his success to what he called, "Mouth to ear advertising." Arney is a spot in the road and difficult to find. "But, people just come," he said, his eyes dancing. "When they get to Freedom they usually stop and ask Marie Boyer at the Shell station where I'm at, and she'll give them directions. Marie," he added with a nod, "is a good neighbor."

Word to ear advertising was exactly how I found him. Yet, some people have been attracted by other forms of advertising. Floyd admitted to using the columns of the Bloomington *Herald Telephone* and *The Prairie Farmer*, and "selling everything I ever advertise." Some of the "everything" included the annual litters from a variety of female hunting hounds he kept for that purpose. "I sell the pups for twenty-five dollars," he said. "And I sell every one. I don't paper my pups, so I sell them for just that amount."

We were seated in what probably was the living room of the Stahl home. Wearing a toboggan pulled down over his ears, a long overcoat buttoned top to bottom, and unlaced rubber boots, Floyd lounged in a spacious overstuffed chair in front of a portable electric space heater, its element rosy red. To one side of that a few lard cans, their lids removed, were bursting with what looked like beef and pork livers and hearts. Food for his hounds, he explained.

"Every once in a while somebody comes along who'd like to chisel me down," Floyd said. "But I try to be nice. Being nice helps you to succeed in business. When I price it, she stays. There's no chiseling here. And I always try to give kids something; a horseshoe, a geode, or something and he'll always come back. I try to be nice," he repeated. "I try to get along with people."

When he was not involved with his collection and people who came to buy pieces of it, Floyd fed cows, pigs, chickens, guineas, geese and ducks, which he raised and were also for sale. During the season he ran a trap line on Fish Creek. At the time of this visit in January 1978, he'd already taken eleven raccoons, eleven possums, two minks, three skunks, one fox, five muskrats and three weasels. In all, he walked two miles a day on the line.

The suggestion that two miles of walking may have been a long distance for a man his age brought a quick smile to Floyd's lips, and an increase in the sparkle in his eyes. "Why I still go out here and split locust poles all day," he said in defense of his personal well being. And he straightaway left the room to return with an armload of chopping axes, a new handle protruding from each of them.

"I've just been putting new handles in these to use on them posts," he said. "And this," he held up a large bulky tool, "this is a beechnut knot maul, I use it for splitting them, too."

The little girl from Sydney who called Floyd's collection "treasures" was Robin, the five year old daughter of his son, Richard, who was with the First National Bank of Chicago, in Sydney, Australia. Richard graduated from Coal City High, and took a bachelor's degree at Purdue. After four years in the Navy, he earned a law degree at Indiana University.

"She just liked to look at it all," Floyd said of his granddaughter. "She'd look at them things and she'd say, 'That's Grandpaw's treasures.' " And he laughed a big laugh.

"Why, there's cross-cuts, and buck-saws, single trees and foot adzes," he said sing-song-like, again gesturing widely. "And branded boxes! Now they'll usually sell for five to eight dollars. I got ten dollars for one. But it was from France.

"There's plows and wooden cultivators," Floyd went on as though participating in a marathon. "And wheat drills and all kinds of horse tools – why, Mister," he shook his head from side to side, "there's a world of stuff out there. Now, I'll tell you, there is."

Floyd then led the way into the zero cold outside where he offered a guided tour of the porch and the outbuildings. "You just won't believe the things I have got," he said.

I resisted. The cold was almost painful to breathe. But before I left him, I had another question. "Where," I asked wonderingly, and also embarrassed by my lack of energy as compared to his, and by his obvious youth in age, "do you find the time?"

"Oh," he said, "I have plenty of time. I even have the time to help my brother, John, farm in the spring and summer."

HARLEY AND VIOLA

Harley Noel had bought himself a spanking new chain saw, but he was not about to get daring with it. Not on your life.

"I aim to take good care of it and not use it too heavy," he told me. And looking out a window from his chair on the enclosed porch of the Noel home on State Road 67 about three miles south of Spencer, Harley added, "Take that tree out there. That's a right smart tree. And I could cut it down and make firewood out of it in no time at all. But," he smiled, "I ain't going to, or I'll run out of work."

There was little danger of that. Harley had twelve acres of woods on the place, and he felt toward them as he did that tree in the front yard of which he spoke. He was not going to dash out there and use the new chain saw too heavy.

This isn't joshing, now, 'cause Harley could make the sawdust fly if he wanted to. It would have been nothing at all for him to hitch the wagon to the tractor and cut enough wood to fill it – the wagon.

"I can cut two or three cords a day," he said, "and not work hard either."

Work is all Harley had ever known. Born on a farm near Freeman, he grew up plowing behind a horse. When he wasn't farming, he was a partner with Dan Neill in a grocery store in Freeman, and again in

Cataract. With the approach in 1923 of chain and larger stores, he decided that country stores were on the way out and no longer for him, and he returned to farming.

But there's more to tell about Harley than work. For one thing – besides being a crackerjack with a chainsaw – he could read the daily newspaper without glasses. Which wasn't a small trick for him. I couldn't have done it at the time. And I was young enough to have been his baby boy. But that's not what I started out to write about him.

I started to write that in three days Harley and the sweet lady who sat on the couch next to me in that long enclosed porch of the Noel home would have marked their seventy-first wedding anniversary. Her name was Viola. She was a Bloomington native who, after the death of her mother, was reared by her uncle, Dan Neill, at Freeman. It was there that Harley met her.

"We were at an ice cream supper at Ben Ranard's place," Harley remembered. "You know, back in those days there was no place else to go. You went to church or you went to an ice cream supper.

"Anyway," he went on teasingly, "we were just kids. She was fifteen. I was robbing the cradle. But I didn't know no better back then."

The "robbing" included courting in a buggy, attending church together, and joining in young people's get-togethers. And, more than not, they were accompanied by another courting couple because parents then believed there was safety in numbers.

"And," Harley pointed out one other parental comfort of those early days, "back in those times you didn't get too far from the house in a buggy."

"Yes," recalled Viola, "we'd go from Freeman to New Hope, or to Hendricksville. But, now, Spencer was a long way off – eight miles. We didn't go there courting."

I wondered aloud what it was like to court in a buggy, not far from home and with another couple, and I winked at Viola and said to Harley, "I suppose it was kind of inconvenient – you know, for kissing?"

Harley laughed. "An old man told me a long time ago that human nature is the same in all generations. And we weren't much different from the kids today," he said.

It was up to me to make what I pleased from that answer and while I did want to give it some thought Harley was talking about winter courting in a buggy. Splashing through a ford on the way to and from church, harness buckles would become a frozen mass of ice, and kissing energies had to be diverted to more necessary matters.

"We'd have to cup those buckles in our hands and blow our hot breath on them to thaw them out to unharness the horse," he said.

Viola laughed at the memory. "I don't think we could do that now," she said.

In later years, after their marriage by a justice of the peace in Spencer, Harley drove a Model-T Ford. There were no harness buckles to freeze up on the thing, but Harley remembered that the radiator sure did a few times.

Harley and Viola told me about their wedding. After they were pronounced man and wife they returned to Freeman. That was it. No honeymoon.

"No one," Harley said, "spent money for a vacation in those days. If they had that much money they bought a house with it."

Four daughters and a son were born to them: Vada McBride of Spencer; Ruth Hartman, Pennsylvania; Zella Strause of Owen County; and Doris Hamilton, also of Spencer. Their son, Kenneth, died at age fifty-seven.

Despite that loss, life had been good to Harley and Viola, and I especially enjoyed hearing Viola say so in her own way.

"It's all been good," she said. "I haven't got anything to complain about. I'm thankful that we got along so well. So many bad things have happened to so many people. But not to us. We're happy. We ought to be happy."

Their many years together had brought them to no great decisions. No earth shaking conclusions. Unless what Harley observed could have been construed as one or the other.

"I believe," he spoke dispassionately from his chair by the window, "that if a man and a woman both believe in God and try to live according to his commandments, they'll get along pretty good.

"Other than that," he continued after a short pause, "life lived is a gradual change. You go along with it, and you automatically change with it."

To which Viola added, "I feel like that's about right, what he said."

Harley and Viola gave up more than two hundred acres and a home they shared on it for forty-seven years to take up residence thirteen years before I met them in the small white frame which sat on thirty acres. Until two winters before our meeting, when the ponds were frozen over, Harley ran a few head of cattle on the place. Without them at this time, Harley spent considerable time sitting by the window that overlooked State Road 67.

"I've sat here more these past two winters than common," he confided. "But," he smiled, "we've got a wood stove in the basement, and I can cut wood for that. And that's why I bought that new chain saw. It's my third one."

There was more to life for Harley and Viola. They would drive to town, to the grocery store, the bank and drug store. They usually went in their 1962 Chevy, which Harley said, "just cackles right along." And with the promise of good weather, they planned to go mushroom hunting. Viola loved mushrooms.

And then there was that anniversary, only a few hours away.

"And if the weather clears up," Harley said of that big day in their lives, "I expect I'll work in the garden."

No big decisions, no earthshaking conclusions.

BIT AT A TIME

While driving along a blacktop that wound from Orleans eastward into Washington County, I was attracted to an ancient house. Just about where Goose Creek emptied into Lost River under an aging, arched, concrete bridge, it stood unpretentious and unassuming. As I neared the place, it became obvious that its eaves were in a state of deterioration, and its paint had atrophied from much time and weather.

A roofed porch spanned its front, and in a swing suspended from the ceiling a woman sat almost unmoving. I turned my car into the driveway and moments later, I was visiting with Ruth Smith. It was our first meeting, yet she made me welcome and invited me to sit down and make myself comfortable in a chair. In a few minutes she began telling me about herself and the old house. She had been living there fifty years. She moved in at the age of thirty and had spent the years unmarried, quietly, unobtrusively feeding chickens, gathering eggs, mowing, gardening, and patiently sitting out the long, cold winters.

There were a few neighbors. But since she had started losing her eyesight almost twenty years earlier, their homes had become too distant to see. The nearby Lost River Baptist Church, where it sat solemnly but handsomely in the "V" of the creek and the river, had also disappeared in the blur. As she spoke, she touched a toe to the porch floor, giving a slight momentum to the swing in which she sat. It was a warm spring day filled with sunshine, yet she wore a red scarf over her gray hair and tied loosely under her wrinkled chin. Had I not found her there, I might never have known that the old house occupied an area once known as Claysville.

"It's always been Claysville, I reckon," she told me. "But I don't know why it was named that, and I don't know when it was named."

Her father, Charles C. Smith, who farmed for many years near Bono, in Lawrence County, retired to the old house long ago. He also bought an adjoining place just to keep his hand in farming.

"This was a farming community then," she observed. "Pretty well-to-do farms, too. The church over yonder had a much bigger congregation then, too, and people used to come to meeting in buggies."

She turned her face into the sun, which she seemed to feel more than see. "You're kind of glad you didn't just sit down and die last winter when a day like this comes along," she smiled a wisp of a smile. She again turned her thoughts to Claysville. "Everything," she said plaintively, "has grown up and changed. Everybody went away, and they won't come back; not to be farmers. People just don't come back to be farmers."

For years her land was tilled and sowed by a man who paid her from the harvest. Despite her failing sight, she marked the last harvest by canning much of what she had received as payment. She was silent for a little while. I noted the strands of gray hair that had escaped from under the red scarf, the creases in her face, the purplish-red of the backs of her frail hands, and the faded blue of her eyes behind dark-rimmed glasses.

She pointed to an impoverished milkhouse. Connected to the porch by a concrete slab walkway, from the middle of which rose a long-handled pump, it was, I heard her say, "where we always kept our fresh milk." Another brief silence and she continued: "We'd pump water for many things there. See, the overflow went that way into that trough and into the milkhouse, where it kept everything so nice and cool. Now the milkhouse is filled with junk."

She was unable to see the pump. Nor could she see the trough. A half century of living in the old house had impressed upon her memory even the location of the loose boards of a graying outbuilding.

At the sound of a truck motor she said, "That'll be the bottle gas man." It was. When the new tank of gas was installed, the bottle gas man presented her with a bill. He knew she couldn't see it. He spoke the price to her.

"If it goes any higher," she said with a sigh, "I'll have to burn corncobs."

"They're high, too," the bottle gas man teased.

"Not if you've got a surplus," she said, nodding toward an outbuilding whose wall she knew from long ago had crumbled, spilling on the ground outside hundreds of rusty corncobs.

After the bottle gas man drove away, she said, "My hens are old as Methuselah now. They're just kind of company for me. And a neighbor friend said the other day that the oldest one does sing kind of nice."

That must have pleased her for she smiled. Then seriously she remarked, "I spent almost twenty dollars for chicken feed the other day. Why, that money would have bought enough eggs to last me the rest of my days, maybe. But they're company, the hens."

She returned her attention to the corncobs. "I shell corn for my hens," she said. "I used to build fires with the cobs, but I don't need them now that I burn bottle gas. But it'll never be like coal; coal kept you warm all over, all the time."

She was silent for a time, touching her toe to the porch floor, gently moving the swing. "I was never lonely when I could see to read," she said at last. "I miss reading. I listen to the radio. If I sit on a stool right in front of the television, I can see a little of it. But I miss reading."

She wondered aloud why she was where she was. Turning her head to look directly at me, she quoted something an uncle would say to her many years ago. "He used to say, 'I don't know why the good Lord won't let us go all at one time, instead of just a little bit at a time.' " She nodded her head, letting the motion speak her agreement.

THE OLD MAN

He said folks went to bed at dark, unless it was a Saturday night and one of the neighbors had a dance at their house.

"We just carried the furniture out of the house, and it was no trouble," he said in recollection. "Hardly anyone owned a rug, and just a few had rocking chairs. There was always a bed, sometimes two, in the front room. It would take a few men only a little bit to get a room ready for dancing."

We were inside a filling station on Persimmon Ridge. He was seated in a rickety old chair. At seventy-four he was short, slight, and slightly stooped. His shoulders appeared pinched together from behind, their tops jutting upward in bony points. He wore glasses under the bill of a railroad engineer's cap whose crown peaked off center. The back of a hand rested on his knee, revealing a labyrinth of creases in his open palm; a palmist's dream.

"There was just as many old people at a dance as there was young ones," he said. "That's who taught the young ones how to dance. There was no round dancing then; we square-danced. And the boys who played music never got a dime."

Fiddlers and banjoists, even guitarists, thrived then, and most of them anxiously awaited the Saturday night get-togethers, he said.

"I remember," he smiled at another memory. "I remember, I was about sixteen, and I was a sort of a (sic) blatherscot. And at one of those dances Franny Frazer said, 'You little devil! Come here!' And she took me through them dances." He shook his head, and he smiled again. "I'll tell you," he smacked his lips, "she made my coattails crack."

Living was more fun back then, he told me. Folks, he said, worked for wages, as they do now, but he said, "We could take a day off and never think a thing about it. You see," he said, "we never had monthly payments to make, and a day off was no problem."

But he hurried on to say, "You have to understand that we didn't take a day off every day. No. We only took one when we had to walk to Bloomfield. And we only went there two, maybe three times a year. No more than that. We had no business there no other times."

Under the heading of business were the Barnum and Bailey Circus, and political orators whose campaign trails reached into the Greene County seat.

"We walked over there one time to listen to a fellow who said he was running for president. Don't remember his name. Don't think he made it either. Don't even remember what he said, he talked for so long. But it always pleasured us to go, to take that long walk, to be off work, and to gather and talk and listen.

"The circus would come once a year for only one day, and they'd put on a show in the evening, and then another one at night. We had many a good time at the circus. All the girls got to go, too. Most of them, anyway. And if you had a horse and buggy you sometimes got to take one home."

He'd turned his hand over and was rubbing the creased palm along his thigh, as though he were soothing an ache.

"It was fun, courting in a buggy," he said with eyes alight. "In a buggy you could tie your lines together and just let your horse go. Then you had both hands free to do what you could, which was more sometimes with some girls than it was at other times with some girls."

He rubbed his thigh some more, and he made the smacking sound with his lips again. "Some of those girls," he sighed. He nodded his head from side to side and he fell silent for a few seconds, savoring a private recollection. "Yes," he said at length, "courting in a buggy was a lot more fun than courting and trying to drive a car all at the same time. And bushes," he exclaimed with a suddenness that broke the tranquility of that nostalgic mood. "We all knew what they were for, and we respected our rights to them. I can remember how fellows would sit straight up in a buggy while his girl went behind one, and I can see still how straight and proper the girls used to sit on the buggy seat when we went. They don't do that anymore either." He suddenly laughed a crackling laugh. "Nobody's got a good use for a bush anymore," he said.

He spoke of bushes some more, and how the long walk to Bloomfield was lined with them. Then he recalled that they didn't always walk to Bloomfield. "Not always," he said. "Sometimes somebody would come along with a hay frame and pick up all the people two horses could pull."

Horses. He'd been around horses all his life, it seemed. He was hostler to thirty-five head of horses when the excavation for the old field house at Indiana University was completed with slip-scrapers and teams, and when the Graham Hotel was built. He coddled those horses in a stable at Tenth and Dunn streets. They were his life, those horses; they provided him with his daily bread, then, too.

"It was a horse that did this to me," he said turning his head. "See. A horse kicked me in the face. My nose was just as flat as a pancake, and my eye was hanging out."

Examination of his aged, wrinkled face revealed no marks, no flattened nose. He'd had those injuries repaired, and if the repair marks were once visible, age had kindly worn them away by the time we met.

He reached into a shirt pocket and brought forth a pack of Camels. He leaned to one side, stretched out one leg, shoved a hand into his pants pocket and produced a jackknife. He juggled the package of cigarettes and knife until a shiny, thin blade glistened in the sunlight that fell around him through a window. He carefully slipped the knife blade into the package top and cut a four-sided opening on one side of the blue tax stamp.

He pressed the back of the blade on the thigh he'd been rubbing and closed it. After returning the knife to his pocket he carefully removed a cigarette from the package and stuck it between his lips.

"It's a habit," he said from around the cigarette that hung from his mouth. "I just got into the habit of opening a package of cigarettes like that and never quit.

"It don't mean nothing," he said.

WORKING ON THE RAILROAD

Down The Track

In his forty-seven years of railroading there had never been linked to his job the romance and dreamy imagination people in general will attach to passing freights in the night, but without men like John Thomas "Tommy" Moore there would be no freights.

"They build the trains that roll on tracks, the trains that train crews move. They are the elite of railroaders," commented Tommy's superior L. C. Love, L & N trainmaster at Bloomington.

Tommy was L & N yardmaster at Bloomington; had been for years. And it was his duty to assemble on paper then oversee the physical composition of freight trains to be moved to near and distant points.

He began his railroading career in 1925. In September of that year he was forced to return to Bloomington High School because he was but fifteen. The following year he parted legally from classes and joined his father, and brother P. J. "Pat" Moore and George W. "Pat" Moore on the old C I & L (Chicago, Indianapolis and Louisville) Railroad, which later was to become the Monon and still later the L & N.

The first years were spent working on rip-track. In 1946 Tommy was moved up to yard switchman with an awesome power over the big engines and long trains.

"They gave him a dollar lantern to tell the trains when to start and stop," explained L & N Claim Agent Russell Jackson, a former engineer.

A former ground-crewman himself, Love recalled, "That lantern was the indicator. Still is. Road crews do what it tells them to do."

Two years after he was made switchman Tommy was promoted to yardmaster.

"There's really not too much you can say about a good man like Tommy," Love mused in recollection of all the years since then, "Except that he's always been here; always been on the job. Wherever he belonged that's where he was. He's a conscientious railroad man. A good railroad man. His life has been devoted to the railroad. He's not been one to lay off. And when he's at home his thoughts and wonderings are with the railroad."

"People who work on the railroad live in a world of their own," said Esther Curry Moore, Tommy's wife. "When they start railroading they have to love it or they wouldn't stay with it. And when it goes through a family like it did his you know they have to love it."

Railroading didn't stop in the Moore family with the two late "Pat" Moores and Tommy. His sons, Larry Joe and John Donald, brakeman and fireman-engineer, respectively, were carrying on the love affair, with the L & N. Another son, George Thomas, was employed in Indianapolis, and a daughter, Phyllis, was associated with Indiana Bell Telephone Company, in Bloomington.

Tommy was a brown-eyed, brown-haired man who watched TV until 10:00 or 10:30 p.m. every night and was up and going at five o'clock every morning. Conversation had to be wrung from him but his reserve was not unpleasant.

"He's quiet," said his wife of forty-four years, "and he reads a lot. He likes sports and he stays young by enjoying life around young people."

Tommy was just days from his sixty-fifth birthday, and he said he didn't feel it. What he did feel was the elation of his retirement from railroading.

Like those freights that pass in the night, Tommy would vanish down the track, where he and Esther would find "The beginning of a new life," Esther promised.

HullCee's Day

It was a moment for a little snuffing and nose-blowing, and it was a time for congratulations and laughter.

This was the last run of HullCee R. Martin, L & N Railroad engineer, who had just stepped down from the big diesel into the arms of his wife, Glenn, the hand-shaking well-wishes of a host of friends, and into retirement.

L. C. Love, trainmaster, presented HullCee with a gold Hamilton wrist watch bearing a fitting inscription on its case.

Above the group, taped under the diesel's cab window opening, a banner made by Oscar Fish read: "The Last Run of H. R. Martin, 50 Yrs Service, 1922-1972."

Road Foreman R. E. Bodie, Claim Agent Russell R. Jackson, Robert Durnal, Bernard Bush, Marvin Hays, Bill Clay, Edgar Davis, Tommy Moore (yard master), Dallas Rood (agent), Margaret Chambers (operator), and several other of HullCee's co-workers through the years were there including his own train crew: Wayne Robison, Roy Hill and Jim Durnal.

HullCee snuffed a couple of times. He dug out a handkerchief from a pocket and blew his nose. Glenn's eyes sparkled from within a gathering of tears.

HullCee's retirement day came on a dark, rainy, Friday afternoon, but at McDoel Yards in Bloomington where he ended his days of throttling the big diesels between Louisville and Lafayette, the atmosphere was bright and cheery.

Inside the yard office there was cake covered with white frosting, and gold lettering which heralded HullCee's achievement.

Here was the last of the steam engineers, the last time Bloomington railroaders would ever say "so-long" to a member of that proud and disappearing band. And those who were present wanted their Hull-Cee to go out right.

HullCee showed his watch around, snuffed and blew again, laughed and ate cake. Then it was time to recall, and relive again the good old days on the railroad. And Glenn, from a long line of railroaders herself, pleasantly deferred to the need for man talk and left the yard office.

A round-robin of recollections shook the yard office with ear-splitting laughter. But it was HullCee's day, and the only recollection which will be repeated here will be one of his.

HullCee was on a switch engine at Midland, near Jasonville in the coal fields of Greene County.

"One of my switchmen came to work this one morning and said he'd taken a physic," HullCee related. "And wherever we moved that engine I noticed he kept looking over to the outhouse at the edge of the yard.

"Well, he got more nervous as time went by, then all of a sudden he jumped off that engine and took out across the tracks for that outhouse. When he got about four feet from that thing he stopped dead in his tracks and clapped his knees together."

HullCee then stood and demonstrated the switchman's position, knees pressed tightly together, hands in mid-air.

"One of the boys called his wife," HullCee continued, "and told her he wanted her to come get him."

"In those days cars had running boards, and when she got there and found out what had happened she wouldn't let him get in the car. She made him ride home on the running board."

HullCee went to work as a railroader for the Monon at age seventeen. After a year in the shops he was made a fireman on a steam engine, and he remained with the engines until his retirement.

"I've had good luck all these years," he said in a serious moment. "And I've had the pleasure of working with fine people, all of them. But I've worked long enough."

"HullCee is a rare individual," Love said. "Never angry, helped everybody, and when it was time for him to be at his job he was there. The railroad always came first with him."

No. 72

The October sky above and the world around us were wet and gray when from up ahead someplace a radiance lit the horizon, and the man at the controls of Monon Freight Train No. 72 knew his next stop would be the Golden Years. No. 72 was northbound from Louisville non-stop to Bloomington. It had slowed some in Bedford, just enough to allow a newspaperman to swing aboard.

It was the last day of the month and Alvin E. Gebhard, age sixty-eight, of Bloomington, was concluding more than fifty-two years of service with the Monon Railroad. His retirement had been scheduled to take effect the next day, so that in subsequent years he and his wife, Gladys, might commemorate their wedding anniversary and his retirement on the same day. They had been married forty-eight years earlier.

"This has been just like any other trip," engineer Gebhard was shouting over the roar of the diesels, "until I got word at Salem that you were coming aboard. Now I feel like that Indiana University football team: I like the smell of roses, too."

At Salem, No. 72 had picked up orders on the fly. Unfolding the thin, green onion skin paper in the dim light of the engine's cab, Gebhard read the clear black handwriting that constituted his last orders: "After fifty years of loyal, conscientious and faithful service you are today handing over the touch to younger hands to run the race you so ably started on March 3, 1915. Congratulations to a well-earned retirement. The man you are and the contribution you have made to the Monon and its employees has made it a better place for all of us to work."

The orders were initialed by Assistant Superintendent of the Southern Division, Richard D. Cantwell. After he folded the green onion skin and stuffed it into a pocket, Gebhard turned his attention to the business at hand. With ninety-three loaded freight cars coming up behind, No. 72 had begun pitching on a downgrade.

As he tightened the reins on the 8,000 diesel horses, Gebhard called out over the noise, "I still have the first set of orders I ever got. This last one kinda choked me up."

After a silent, thoughtful moment he added, "I don't regret any of my years with the Monon. It was a lot of hard work, and a lot of it was enjoyable. But it can't go on forever, and I don't want to stay on until I get down. I want to fish and have fun."

As he spoke, a section crew waved from the side of the railbed. The word must have been passed up and down the Monon that this was Gebhard's last trip. Either that or No. 72 must have had that Golden-Years-Bound look about it, for from then on it seemed that everyone we passed waved.

Gebhard had begun his railroading career as a roundhouse employee. His last forty-four years were spent in firing and ramrodding engines. He took one leave of absence in 1917 to 1918 to serve with the Army during World War I.

On his feet he stood about an inch under six-feet, and he admitted to about two-hundred pounds. Light blue eyes seemed always to be smiling, and a full pink and white face became brighter when he spoke. A member of two committees of the North Central Church of Christ, he seemed happy that retirement would give him more time to give to the church. Railroaders, he complained, don't have much time for anything except their work. In spite of that and his age, he had a youthful look about him.

"I quit smoking when I was fifty years old," he said. "I wouldn't be alive today if I hadn't. It was killing me. The doctor told me I had better slow up, but you can't slow up when it comes to smoking."

As No. 72 rumbled toward its destination, fireman Lester Johnson, of Bedford, sat at a window opening on the opposite side of the cab looking far off across the passing hills. Russell Jackson, Trainmaster and Road Foreman of Engineers, sat in front of him. Jackson had come to spend these last few hours with an old friend and fellow employee.

"We're going to take it easy now," Gebhard said loud enough to be heard over the rumble and roar of the diesel. "When we get tired, we'll go fishing. I have a good friend down in Florida, and we can spend some summers in Colorado."

As he spoke, he pulled on the whistle cord. No. 72 was swaying and banging its way into the Bloomington railroad yards and the end of Gebhard's last run. Railroad friends were waiting to shake hands and to congratulate him, and to bid him farewell.

And Gladys was waiting to take him home from there for the last time.

A Friendly Toot

She called it "our little outing", and she flashed a smile across the table to her husband who was seated in the booth opposite her. "We're here every day," she continued. "We like to get out for a little while. It makes everything more pleasant."

I tried to remember our first meeting. I couldn't. She helped me. "The Variety Store," she said.

Spencer's Variety Store was equipped with a fountain then, and a counter and booths. Mildred and Fillmore England were still living out in the county, in their "dream home" they'd built in 1958. They used to come to town even then on their little outings.

There was a nest of happy Baptists who operated the Variety Store for Jack Money then: Pauline

Gross, Helen Summerlot, Lillian Ranard, Mable Watkins and Mary Gentry.

They'd talk a lot about their church, those ladies, and the services held there, and what their minister said. They'd talk about those things, those ladies, but only some of the time. There were other topics, and, as someone once remembered, "You could catch up on the news there – news that was news."

The fountain in the Variety Store was a duplicate of the one in the drug store, which was practically next door. And, judging from what Jack told me once, it was a duplicate of the loss suffered by that one. So he shut it down. When he did, the Variety Store fountain bunch began lighting at the drug store's fountain.

It was there that I encountered the Englands and, after Mildred's kind gesture, began remembering the Variety Store fountain and our previous meeting there.

More precisely, it was Lewis Loser who brought about this more recent meeting. Seated next to him at the counter I overheard him say to the Englands: "My engineer was late last night," and he added something about "blowing his whistle."

Curious, I asked Lew what he was talking about. This is what I learned.

While Paul "Polly" Fulk was throttling freight-pulling engines over that section of the Pennsylvania road, and later the Penn-Central (now Conrail) road, that runs through Spencer, he'd yank the whistle cord a couple of times as he passed Lew's house at 135 West Franklin Street.

Polly at this time was retired. The man who had been his fireman, and who always waved at Lew, was then the engineer on that run. He resumed Polly's tooting when he passed Lew's house. His fireman, the man who took his place, flashed a light at Lew when they passed.

There was nothing thrilling about all this, I know. But every time that train's whistle was tooted it was also heard by the Englands, who lived across the tracks from Lew at 59 South Montgomery Street. The tooting was not meant for them, it was a gesture of friendship extended to Lew.

When he heard that tooting, Lew could look at his watch and check the train's time – on time, early or late? Whichever it may have been didn't matter a whole lot, but it did give Lew something to do, and something to mention when he stopped at the soda fountain the next day. And he would add something personal about the engineer to whatever he said, such as "He has a steady hand on that throttle. Steadier than most." And he might have added to that, "Polly had a steady hand on that throttle, too. Steadier than most."

Like I said, the Englands – Fillmore and Mildred – also heard the tooting whistle of the passing train (as did most of the town), which was meant for Lew. And it gave them the opportunity, depending on which way the train was traveling, to remark, "Here he comes," or, "There he goes." Sometimes they acknowledged the tooting by saying, "Here he is," or "Here he goes."

Fillmore was an engineer for the same road. He retired after forty-two years of service. He was always steady on the throttle. After he and Mildred built their dream home twenty years earlier they began living there happily ever after. When Mildred had sufficiently refreshed my memory on their identity, I recalled some things about that home as I had learned in our first meeting so many years earlier at the soda fountain at the Variety Store.

Fillmore was just about seventy-five then, still spry, still quite active. I remembered that he sat there smiling as Mildred recounted an experience they had shared with a family of raccoons. The mother raccoon would settle her young safely in a tree, then make her way to a large window. There she'd rap for attention. If one of her young dared to come down the tree she would spank it, and the young one, obeying her, would return to the tree.

The mother raccoon continued her rapping until she was fed by Fillmore or Mildred. After eating her fill, she would then return to her family, lead them down the trunk of the tree, and conduct them into the surrounding woodlands.

There were other wild things around that home, including lovely flowers and trees. There was also something wild, and rare, about the very air they breathed. It was all so wonderful. When you consider that they had spent most of their lives in Indianapolis, convenient to Fillmore's job, rural Owen County was heavenly, even for people their age. As I said, they took time for their outings even then. It all ended too soon.

Fillmore suffered a broken leg when their car slipped out of gear and rolled back over him from its parking place at home. They sold the country place and moved to town, where they could be nearer to the care he needed, and to the help either of them might have needed in the future. Three years later, Fillmore suffered a stroke. He recovered enough so that together, with Mildred's help, they could still have their little afternoon outings at the drug store soda fountain.

They were smiling people, pleasant people. She ordered a diet drink, Fillmore would have a single dip of chocolate ice cream. They'd visit with folks in the booths or at the fountain. When they finished their drink and ice cream, Mildred helped Fillmore to his feet, he'd take her arm, and they'd leave. Still smiling, still pleasant.

Like I said, there is nothing thrilling about all this. Lew didn't even know the name of the engineer who tooted the whistle at him every time he passed Lew's house. Neither did Fillmore and Mildred know his name. If they did they could have said, "Here comes Jack," instead of "Here he comes," or, "There goes Jim," instead of, "There he goes."

When you're seventy-nine, like Lew, and eighty-five, like Fillmore, life doesn't have to be thrilling. However, a little thing like the friendly toot of an engine's whistle can be very important, as it was for Lew. It could be just as important to you (although it's not tooted especially for you) if you, like the Englands, would always hear it.

'Spotty'

You couldn't have known him for he lived at another time in another place, a placed called Cementville, on the old Monon Railroad. Because he was a little white fellow with black spots he was called "Spotty."

And because he was of unknown ancestry, he was probably viewed by some as a mongrel. No matter. He was to those who knew him best a very special kind of creature; and he shared a unique love affair with them – the crew of the local freight train.

When the local was not chugging and shissing in and out of the cement plant in the small Indiana community, Spotty romped the beautiful surrounding hills and splashed in the cool waters of a nearby picturesque creek that runs parallel to the railroad there.

The high point of his day was the arrival of the local which Spotty never failed to meet. He recognized the clanking chug-chug sound of the old steam locomotive as it came into Cementville to set off and pick up cars.

It wasn't the sound of any railroad locomotive that attracted Spotty. On the contrary. The mainline trains came and went, day and night, and none ever drew his interest. Yet, when he heard the local, that one engine, he recognized its sound. And he'd stop whatever he was doing and run at breakneck speed to meet its crew, his friends.

Spotty may have been aided in his recognition of the local and its crew by the locomotive's whistle. As the freight neared the cement plant the engineer would send four loud blasts through the whistle, shattering the day around it. Hoo-o-o-t! Hoo-o-o-t! Hoo-o-o-t! Hoo-o-o-t! The engineer would pull the whistle cord. And when the rumbling, clanking freight came to a halt Spotty would be there at the end of the train – waiting for the crew to descend the caboose.

Tail wagging, quivering in every muscle, eyes bright and seeking, he awaited their appearance from the funny looking railroad car. At last he'd see his railroader friends. He'd jump and bark almost hysterically as they climbed down from the caboose, expressing in the only way he knew how his joy at seeing again the big, rough men in overalls and strange-looking caps.

Spotty loved them. It might be safe to say they loved him. With caring hands, they fed him food from their lunch boxes. He wagged his tail, his small hips, in gratitude. His little heart thump-thumped in appreciation. And there emitted from his small throat, as he ate, tiny sounds of thanksgiving.

At the termination of this daily ritual, there began the ceremony of following the railroaders and their train around as they went about switching hopper cars. The railroaders spoke to him, called to him, and he replied with yaps and barks, and a wagging tail.

When the train moved into the plant to switch hoppers inside the building, Spotty knew the biggest thrill of the day. He was lifted to the engine's cab where he rode on the lap of the engineer or the fireman, looking out the cab window, the proudest little being in the world. On the ground inside the plant he would have another opportunity to visit with the train crew.

While the men worked inside, Spotty liked to explore the plant. It offered an abundance of places for him to stick his snout. And he seemed to know that since he was a friend to the men on the local, the gruff plant guard would not run him off.

He also knew when the fun was over for the day, for as soon as the engine coupled into the rest of the train he would bark a goodbye and run off to play and sleep until the next day. Until he heard the four blasts of the engine's steam whistle signalling the local's return, and the return of his railroader friends, he usually stayed away from the tracks.

The routine, the relationship, continued for years. Always the four blasts from the locomotive's whistle. Always the same affection from the train's crew. Always the same love returned by Spotty. He met them every day and was with them two hours or more while they worked at the cement plant. He wasn't a very pretty creature, but the big railroaders saw a beauty in him. And he didn't mind if they were tall or short, fat or skinny, or otherwise; he loved them.

One cold winter's day when the ground was covered with three inches of snow, the local chug-chugged into Cementville. The engineer gave four solid pulls on the locomotive's steam whistle. Hoo-o-o-t! Hoo-o-o-t! Hoo-o-o-t! Hoo-o-o-t! But when the freight came to a stop, Spotty was not at his usual place outside the caboose awaiting his friends and the treats they had for him.

A crewman carrying a bag of food for Spotty walked the tracks calling his name. Spotty did not answer. Then the crewman saw something, a small mound in the snow a few feet from the right of way. It was Spotty. An inch of snow covered his frozen little body. He was lying facing the tracks as though he had been waiting for his friends when death overtook him.

With loving hands, the railroaders tenderly lifted the frozen body of their spotted little friend. They wrapped it carefully in a blanket, and they buried it in the frozen ground between the main line and the spur that goes into the cement plant. Later they placed a stone marker on the grave. The inscription read: Spotty, 1-6-1939.

No, you couldn't have known him, for he lived at another time in another place. But you know of him now, and I hope you like what you know.

THE JACKSON ODYSSEY

Clearly the ketch *Carla Mia* was in serious trouble. Her skipper, W. Carl Jackson, Indiana University Dean Of Libraries, who was singlehanding her across the Atlantic Ocean from Marblehead, Massachusetts, to Hampton, England, became aware of it with heart-stopping suddenness. On her fourth night out to sea, after a month of abortive attempts to get underway, the ketch's lower shrouds, halyards, and sheets lay in a tangle on her deck and trailing over her side.

A weary, two-dollar bolt, overlooked by workmen in the refitting of the boat, had severed and with a hair-raising clatter and bang the rigging had slammed down. The sails also plummeted to the deck when Jackson, fearful the mast might buckle, rushed to release their halyards. In a single moment of illumination from the lofty spreader lights, before a new marine battery unexplainably lost its power and plunged man and boat into the pitch-black of a moonless night, Jackson's usual calm was staggered by the enormity of the calamity.

Until the latest adversity overtook her, the thirty-foot ketch had been making steady way against twenty-foot seas, pushed before a strong wind. Now, her forward motion gone, and in the darkness of the Atlantic night, the *Carla Mia* was broaching dangerously. With an iciness born of genuine fear, her

W. CARL JACKSON
Dean Of Indiana University Libraries

skipper became suddenly aware of the boat's violent pitching and rolling, and of the prospect of the weakened mast buckling and punching a hole in the hull. He dove into the cabin and turned on the switch that would activate the boat's emergency locator beacon. Then he hastily gathered up his sextant, field glasses, two jugs of drinking water, wool clothing and other articles he thought he would need if he had to abandon the small boat. Back on deck, he saw his situation in better perspective. The boat's need of relief from the violent pounding seas seemed urgent. In order to give it relief, if he could, he needed light to see what he was doing. Jackson again rushed below and started the diesel auxiliary which, in turn, would supply power to a backup lighting system.

Returning to the deck, he was somewhat calmed by the brightness of the spreader lights. But then he was aware of movement. He was certain he had put the engine in neutral, but he could feel the boat's forward motion. The *Carla Mia* was making way, pushed by the diesel's revolving prop. The twisted mass of shrouds, sheets and halyards trailing over the side could foul the turning prop, further disabling the boat. Once more he dove below. Before he could reach the engine switch, his fears had crystallized. The trailing mass had wound around the prop shaft, strangling the diesel into an ominous silence. The *Carla Mia* now lay crippled somewhere in the Atlantic Ocean. It was a moment for panic, however fleeting, and in that briefness of time, the changes of fortune of a man and his sailboat retraced themselves in Jackson's mind.

It began as a dream many years earlier. When he was a small boy in Beverly, Massachusetts, Jackson built small sailboats from scraps of lumber. He caulked them with tar taken from tacky street surfaces and sailed them in the bay. From these boyhood adventures a more daring one – singlehanding the Atlantic – began to take shape. The early death of his mother, when he was seven, and the later serious injury of his barnstorming pilot father, became the first of many delays in the realization of that dream. The beginning of World War II found him still a young man, and still adventurous. Disappointed that he could not meet the physical requirements to become a pilot, he volunteered for the newly organized 82nd Airborne Division. He served in the European Theater of Operations, concluding those dangerous paratrooper years at the Battle of the Bulge, in 1945.

Three years later, he married Mary Elisabeth Lett, and in that same year entered Florida State University, where in 1951 he took a B. A. degree in history. The following year he won an M.A. there in library science. From then until 1973, when he became dean of libraries at Indiana University in Bloomington, Indiana, Jackson was employed on the staffs at universities in Tennessee, Iowa, Minnesota, Colorado and Pennsylvania. He also was consultant to others all over the United States, and in some foreign countries. Other professional activities took him on international travels, and his collection of memberships in professional organizations grew. All conspired to delay the consummation of the aging dream of sailing the Atlantic. Still, wherever he was, Jackson managed to find time for his boyhood love. While in Bloomington, he was an active, competitive member of the Bloomington Yacht Club at Lake Lemon, and the Lake Monroe Sailing Association at Moores Creek.

One day Jackson was aware of a gnawing that steadily increased in intensity. He was more than fifty years old. If his dream of sailing the Atlantic was ever to become more than that, he counseled himself, he should set about doing it soon, or forget it. The latter was out of the question, and early in 1974, Jackson began shopping the east coast for a boat. One he preferred for his adventure was financially out of his reach. Seeking all the boat his money could buy, he settled, in July of 1977, for a thirty-foot Allied Sea Wind ketch, sister boat to the Apogee, first of its kind to circumnavigate the world. Thus began the Jackson Odyssey.

He at once began familiarizing himself with the boat. He arranged with a reputable boatyard to make some twenty-five to thirty modifications and repairs. He named the boat after his daughter, an only child born to the Jacksons in 1962. Christening it the *Carla Mia*, he himself shaped and carved the name on large wooden plates and attached them port and starboard to the boat's doghouse. He registered Louisville, Kentucky, on the Ohio River, as its port of hail and had the name painted on her stern. And last of all, after twenty-eight years of steady work, Jackson applied for and received a ninety-day administrative leave, scheduled to begin June 1, 1978.

His plans called for loading the *Carla Mia* with the necessary stores, and casting off immediately. Above all else, getting out to sea was what Jackson believed he needed. He felt desperate to get away from the routine and sedentary life required of his work; he was burned out, fatigued. Yet, when Elisabeth accompanied him to the *Carla Mia's* berth on Chesapeake Bay to see him off, Jackson entertained mixed feelings. He was happy to be starting out on his long-dreamed adventure, happy to be getting away from the pressures of his job, but sad, even reluctant, to be leaving his wife. Neither he nor Elisabeth was aware of it then, but they were not to be separated for a while, not yet.

When they arrived at the *Carla Mia* early in June, Jackson, to his dismay, discovered that much of the work he had paid to have done had to be redone. Because of poor workmanship, he now found himself spending most of the month of June – some of his best sailing days, as he would say later – at dockside in the U.S. making the repairs himself. To say the very least, he felt let down. But he was determined to set sail across the Atlantic, and he worked long and tirelessly to correct the shoddy work.

Elisabeth, meanwhile, became an invaluable assistant. While the skipper of the *Carla Mia* labored from dawn until dark repairing his boat, she became his "gofor," shopping for parts and other needs. She also bought groceries and other supplies her husband would take on his journey, packing and sealing them in waterproof plastics and storing them aboard. Finally, on June 21, Jackson cast off and set sail for Annapolis, where he would buy additional parts and equipment for his boat before setting sail eastward across the Atlantic. Elisabeth motored up to Annapolis, where she and her husband would say their good-byes on June 23, before she returned to their home in Bloomington.

Jackson then sailed northward to Cape May, where he made his first offshore trial run. For three days the *Carla Mia* was pounded by gales before her skipper, satisfied that his boat was seaworthy, set a course for Montauk Point, at the northern tip of Long Island. When the ketch raised the lighthouse on her bow, Jackson was thrilled to learn that his navigation was flawless. He remembered his final test score at navigation school – one hundred out of a possible one hundred points. He put the wheel over and swung the ketch northward, passing Block Island and continuing on to Marblehead. In passing Buzzard's Bay, he placed a telephone call over his marine radio to Elisabeth. The *thirteenth* boater in line, Jackson waited patiently, listening to other mariners' conversations as their voices droned over the set. One by one they completed their calls until Jackson had moved up to sixth place in the waiting line. Then his radio, an expensive, reputable American make, went dead. At Marblehead, a technician worked on it for three hours. Although he was unable to repair it, he charged Jackson fifty-eight dollars for his labor.

Jackson was aware of a growing dismay. Only hours away from his departure for England, and more than a third of his leave already used up, he could feel himself falling into a state of marina malaise. He was terribly driven to get to sea, and to get clear of the annoyances of little things gone wrong, but at almost every turn finding himself thwarted by newer and newer problems.

By this time the hapless sailor was also suspicious of the ketch's steering vane. The equivalent of an automatic pilot, it was designed to free him from the helm and allow him to rest and to sleep. He was also aware of rising doubts about the timing now left him for the transatlantic crossing – was it not too late in the season? Early in the spring he had confided to Elisabeth that a late June or early July departure might be the wrong time. Yet, thus far, it was not the weather that had been his nemesis; the culprit was poor workmanship by people who simply were not concerned or committed enough to do their jobs properly.

Jackson was aware of something else, too, or at least thought he was. He found himself wondering if some mysterious force, perhaps, "Someone out there," didn't want him to make the solo crossing. But enough of that, he told himself. With thirty-seven days of his ninety day leave already used up, he said to himself, "The heck with the radio, the heck with it all," and on July 8 the beleaguered skipper set sail on the three thousand mile journey across the Atlantic. He had plotted a course that would keep the *Carla Mia* south of the shipping lanes north of the Azores. His course would also keep him south of the Icelandic Low, which is also very prominent and produces extreme storms, heavy seas and gales. Making way toward the east end of this corridor, he would sail up the United States and Canadian coasts, avoiding Cape Sable and its notorious fogs – or so he thought.

The daring sailor had tried to keep his transatlantic venture a secret; his reason being simple and honest. He wasn't sure he had the courage to challenge the Atlantic alone in a thirty-foot sailboat. But if he chickened out, as he himself feared such a possibility, he was too proud to have his failure made public, perhaps even written in the newspapers. He felt strongly that his attempt to singlehand the *Carla Mia* to Hampton, England, was his show, and only his. He wanted to prove nothing to the world, only to himself, that he could make his dream come true. He was disturbed then, when he telephoned from Marblehead to his home in Bloomington, to learn that his secret was out.

Elisabeth had gone shopping and was not at home and Jackson spoke with his daughter, Carla, then a student at South High School. During their conversation she told him there had been a story about him on the front page of the daily newspaper. Jackson was not aware, and Carla had failed to inform him, that the secret slipped out when she proudly nominated him for the newspaper's "Annual Greatest Father of the Year" contest. And he was unable to restrain his annoyance at the news.

Now, as he tried to assess the damage and his predicament aboard the disabled *Carla Mia* in the pitch-black of a midnight ocean, Jackson remembered with remorse his spontaneous irritation at what his daughter had divulged. He believed that, in his response to her words, he had been cruel to Carla. He heard the echo of his voice, the words he had spoken into the telephone to her: "Oh, Carla, why did you tell them?" He believed he had burdened her with unnecessary guilt, and his regret at this moment of travail at sea was profound. He wished that he could say to her, "I'm sorry, forgive me." Had he been able to read his daughter's letter nominating him the greatest father because of her love for him, and her pride in him, the remorse he suffered might have been greater, but the terrible panic inside him might have been soothed.

Because of zero visibility that cold midnight, Jackson could not see the tangle of sails and halyards on the deck of the *Carla Mia*. He knew the mess was there. He had seen them briefly before double disaster had darkened the spreader lights above the deck. He also had time to see the mast, weakened by the loss of two of its supports, its thirty-two feet of length in danger of buckling, as he would say later, "Doing a belly dance." He had to take steps to save his boat.

His eyes somewhat adjusted to the darkness by this time, he fashioned a monkey fist – a large knot – at the end of one of many extra ropes with which he had supplied the *Carla Mia*. He heaved it over the port spreader – the crosspiece on the mast – and pulled it down around the mast and fastened it to a deckplate. He passed the other end of the rope through the winch on the mast and back to the cockpit, where he cranked the winch, tightening the line to the spreader. As he continued to work the winch, the mast settled on its base, and it held under the makeshift repair. Under the best of conditions, the task would have been demanding. In the darkness of an Atlantic night, on a disabled boat pitching and heaving in twenty-foot seas, it had been exhausting.

When it was finished, Jackson was aware that much time had passed. For the moment he felt safe, but he dared not underestimate the seriousness of his predicament. He longed desperately for daybreak, when he might better determine his boat's condition and make what repairs he could.

Despite his fears, he was still angrily cognizant of this being his second start on his long sea voyage. He remembered the first, when he and Elisabeth arrived on Chesapeake Bay to pick up the *Carla Mia* at the boatyard. Had the boat been repaired as he had ordered, he would have been on his way to England in early June. And this time, delayed by one month, he had set out from Marblehead only four days ago.

Jackson remembered that afternoon. It was about three o'clock, and his lifelong dream was at last coming true. He tried to remember his feelings. Dreaming of sailing and actually sailing are two separate activities, and he had done both for years. But that afternoon was different. He knew he was no longer dreaming, no longer sailing the waters of an inland lake. Dreaming and romance could no longer be the entertainments of his mind.

Filled with optimism and hope, he had cast off the sailboat's lines and pointed her eastward into reality. Abaft the taffrail the coast of the United States soon faded from the horizon, and he knew that he was at last committed to the challenges of a mighty ocean.

While in Marblehead, he had tried to ignore the reports of missing yachts then being searched for by the U.S. Coast Guard. He told himself that no matter the size of a yacht, no matter the number of crew, boats capsize, and boats go down. He told himself that he was aware that misfortune could strike at any time, in any form and that it was the character of the challenge he had accepted.

He had faced challenges before. Jumping with the 82nd Airborne Division into unknown World War II beachheads, for example. Pinned down by artillery fire in the Battle of the Bulge, when his blood turned to water. Carried out of the Bulge in February, 1945, with frozen feet and other injuries. He had faced misfortune as a boy at the time of his mother's death, and after his barnstorming pilot father was injured. Alone, and without help, he learned to provide for himself. Those were shattering experiences, as were others in his life. Because he never saw himself as a courageous person, each had left its mark on him.

In more recent years, Jackson had seen himself only as a middle-aged librarian, the product of a variety of backgrounds. Still, as he had done as a boy, and later as a young man, he continued in rare moments to still see himself in a romantic cast, involved in an adventurous life. Secretly he yearned to become a denizen of the coast of Maine, in Jonesport, perhaps, operating his own lobster boat and not being responsible to anyone. In more rational moments, he felt satisfied with life in Bloomington. He was pleased with his position. But he believed that at some point he wanted to be a librarian, and have more time for himself and his family, and some time in which to write. He wished to be able, some day, to spend less time amid the acrimonies that often belabor administrative society. He hoped some day to see an end to human violence and maiming, and to witness an acceptance by the human race of tolerance, understanding and sympathy. And he hoped, ideally, that one day all humans would be kind and loving to one another.

Outbound from Marblehead that first afternoon, the wind was brisk at fifteen miles an hour. Toward late evening Jackson had turned the helm over to the steering vane and went below to rest. He would soon be in the middle of the busy shipping lanes out of Boston, and he wanted to be rested for the long night's vigil. While he slept, a heavy fog had moved in. He awakened drenched, and everywhere he looked on the *Carla Mia* the boat was dripping as though from a rainstorm.

The fog remained with man and boat for the four days before the fateful midnight mishap from which he was now trying to recover. Moisture clung to everything; it ran down everything, dripped on everything. Jackson, himself, was aware of a claustrophobic sensation, of being imprisoned in the cold, clammy, blinding fog.

Suddenly, he was alert to another dimension in fear. From out of the thick fog, it came – BOOM! BOOM! With an emptiness in the pit of his stomach, Jackson saw himself in the middle of a naval gunnery range! Unable to see, unable to be seen, he resorted to all he had left to reveal his presence, a canned-air horn, and his voice. He gave the horn a blast. He shouted, "Hey, Navy! I'm here! I'm here, Navy!" He released more compressed air into the horn to sound another blast into the pea soup fog and on its way to whoever was firing those big guns so close to him and the *Carla Mia*.

The firing stopped. Jackson breathed a sigh of relief. The fog stayed and, if anything, got thicker.

The day, the night, passed. The next day the heavy naval guns resumed. BOOM! BOOM! Jackson's consternation increased. Why were they following him in the fog? Had they not heard his signals the previous day? His shouts? It was not until he heard similar sounds the third day at sea that he was able to deduce that, in fear for his life in the blinding fog, he had resorted to fantasy. Although he was unable to see or hear a plane, he had allowed himself to be victimized by sonic booms.

On his fourth night at sea, with the darkness hiding the evidence of the calamity that had struck his boat, Jackson's thoughts were interrupted by lesser but more ominous sounds than the sonic booms. Seas running twenty-feet in height were pounding the ketch, and its skipper feared that any one of the big waves might smash the hull of the small boat. With agonizing slowness, the remainder of the frightening night passed.

At break of day, the seas and fog subsided. Surveying the deck of the *Carla Mia*, the fallen shrouds, sails, the lines trailing over the boat's side to its propeller, where they were snarled like gripping tentacles, Jackson reached a decision that turned his blood to ice. He would lower himself over the side to unsnarl the prop. He knew that a grave, a deep watery grave, awaited his slightest mistake. He thought about the date, the early hours of July 12. Had he been able to follow the sailing schedule he had set for himself, he might well have found himself and his boat already across the Atlantic and docked at Hampton, England.

Unfortunately, that was not so; and in the earliest light of that day, Jackson studied his dilemma and how best to overcome it. Halyards and sheets had slipped further over the side during the night. He wondered if just one, or more, had become entangled in the boat's propeller. Of one thing he was certain, whatever the problem, it would not fix itself. He would have to go down into the sea and repair it himself. He was grateful that from the moment of the mishap, the boat's emergency locator beacon had been sending out signals for help. During the long night he had hoped it would be heard by planes or rescue ships.

Fortunately, the murky fog that had dogged the *Carla Mia* for four days had lifted with the new dawn. But now, now that he searched the sky and horizon, there was no sign that anyone had heard. While the emergency locator continued sending out its signal, Jackson, resigned to whatever fate awaited him, knew that regaining control of his boat was solely up to him. He was grateful that the seas had calmed, but dare he risk raising sail and putting a strain on the weakened mast? He opted to unfoul the boat's prop. But how? There was only one way, and that was to go over the side. With the lifting of the fog, the seas had fallen off.

The past month had been a trying one for the fifty-five year old skipper, and the last four days, and especially the previous night, had further wearied him. Did he have the strength to withstand the physical demands that lay ahead?

Whether he did or did not, Jackson knew that he must either go over the side or continue to lie dangerously crippled in the water. Yet, he admitted to himself, he was afraid. He knew that, once in the water, it would be difficult to climb back into the boat. He knew, too, that in extreme circumstances, even the best planned intentions somehow go awry, and serious mistakes are committed.

Jackson spent nearly an hour thinking on these things, and in his mind he itemized everything that could go wrong with what he was planning to do. It didn't occur to him that he might not have to go over the side; he knew only that if the weather worsened and the seas became violent he would be in sore need of power – the *Carla Mia's* diesel auxiliary. He admitted something else to himself – if he waited too long he would not have the courage to go over the side to try to unfoul the prop, especially in heavy winds and turbulent seas.

He had prepared for an unusual event. A boarding ladder had been installed on each side of the cockpit at the stern quarters. While neither could be reached from the water, each trailed a rope that could be grasped by someone in the water, and a solid pull would bring the ladders down within reach. Jackson had included the ladders as part of the boat's standard equipment because he had heard and read of so many singlehanders washed overboard by a swamping sea, or swept overboard by a wildly shifting boom. Although he wore a safety harness to protect himself from such a mishap, he knew those probabilities still were very real aboard a sailboat, and that he could be dragged and drowned behind his own boat.

Having tested the efficiency of the ladders, he was sure they would serve his need. But he had never tried to use them while he was fatigued; and he wondered with growing fear if he would have the strength to climb them while he was thus incapacitated. He would have to chance it.

Committed to that knowledge, the skipper of the *Carla Mia* pumped up the boat's rubber dinghy, securely lashed it to the boat with two ropes, and put it over the side. Satisfying himself that his safety harness was secure, he then climbed down the starboard ladder and lowered himself into the dinghy. At that point, he used another line to tether himself to the boat. From there he studied the transom, and he observed another danger. The calm seas were not so calm after all. In time with the waves that struck her, the *Carla Mia's* stern was rising out of the water and falling back at regular intervals. Were he to be caught under it as it fell with the motion of the waves, he stood in danger of sustaining a cracked skull, or at least being knocked unconscious and possibly into the water. It was under the rising and falling transom that the fouled prop was located. The danger gave Jackson moment for pause. The *Carla Mia* was equipped with an outboard rudder, complete with stout pegs on either side, which, with lines properly attached, could have been used for emergency steering.

In the midst of his hesitation, Jackson's next move became clear to him. Timidly, because he was also thinking of sharks suddenly appearing to devour him, he let himself out of the dinghy and into the water. He then got a grip on the large rudder and clambered up on the pegs. He clung there for more than an hour, riding the rising and falling stern of the ketch as though it was a bucking bronco. When it rose, his head was out of the water. When it fell, his entire body was under water. As he jockeyed the rudder, he somehow managed to grasp the lines that ensnarled the prop. He sorted them in his mind as he worked to remove them from the prop, and he sadly concluded from the precariousness of his position that he and the *Carla Mia* were "in a damn mess."

At last he was able to leave the hazardous perch and return to the pitching dinghy. Looking up at a boarding ladder, he determined to learn if he could climb it in a state of exhaustion. He slowly lowered himself from the dinghy into the water and slowly, painfully, climbed the ladder to the sailboat's cockpit. The exertion nearly did him in and, once there, he just sat and trembled for more than an hour, until he could regain his strength and composure. It was in those long minutes that the skipper of the *Carla Mia* realized that in all his years, regardless of other dangers he had faced, he had never before been so scared. But was it fear? He tried to sort that sensation from the shock and the fatigue, and from the exultation and joy he knew at having freed the crippled *Carla Mia*, and he could not.

When at last he was again in control of himself, Jackson did a strange thing. He returned to the dinghy, and with a brand new Konica 35mm camera that he bought especially for his adventure, he took photographs of the stern of the boat. Then he climbed back aboard and pulled in the dinghy.

The *Carla Mia,* by this time, had been lying without sail or auxiliary power for eighteen hours. Now, with the mast jury-rigged and the prop unfouled, and no one had come to Jackson's rescue, there was no reason for remaining in that position. He switched off the emergency locator beacon, set a new course for the *Carla Mia*, and set sail for Nova Scotia for repairs.

Wary of the jury-rigged mast, Jackson, nevertheless, raised aloft a storm trisail. He then unfurled the Genoa foresail about halfway, and hoisted the mizzen sail. With a good wind out of the west, the *Carla Mia* began making a brisk northwest passage. The wind held through the night and the ketch sailed on without incident. Next morning, Jackson sighted a ship. He broke out his flare gun, loaded it, and pulled the trigger. The gun failed.

Fortunately, Jackson, at this time, needed no help. He wished only to get a message out on the ship's radio to anyone who might have heard his emergency locator beacon. He wanted to say that he was all right

THE CRIPPLED *CARLA MIA*.
(Shot From The Dinghy)

and heading for port under his own power, and any rescue proceedings should be canceled. He put the flare gun aside and dug out a flashlight and blinked an SOS in the direction of the ship. It passed on, giving no indication the signal had been seen.

The rest of that day passed without further event. On the morning of the 15th, Jackson's attention was drawn to the flight overhead of a piston-driven airplane. He believed it to be a search plane. When the pilot flew several miles south of the ketch's position before circling and leaving the area, Jackson concluded it was a fishery patrol plane.

Later that morning, a Canadian search and rescue plane spotted the *Carla Mia*, and it dropped flares in the direction of land – a direction Jackson already knew and in which he was sailing – and left.

Shortly after that, an American search and rescue plane appeared. It dropped a huge canister, then began a circling flight that would last for more than three hours.

After dropping sail and heaving to, Jackson struggled with the large canister for what seemed an eternity. At last, almost in total exhaustion, he was able to pull it aboard. Freeing it from its drogue chutes, tugging at what seemed tons of packing material from its interior, he at last found its contents – a small two-way radio with written instructions for its use. The radio was faulty – it did not work.

Jackson then put the *Carla Mia* back on a course for Nova Scotia. The wind had fallen off, but the boat could still make way. Then, seemingly from out of the sea around him, he became aware of a strange rumbling. It continued for a long time. Suddenly, he saw its source – a huge gray mass on the horizon, and coming his way. Charging at full speed, it suddenly took the shape of a warship. Veering off at the last moment, the Canadian cutter *Daring* came alongside the sailboat. Without question or introduction, a young officer on her deck informed the skipper of the smaller boat that he would be taken in tow. A huge rope was passed over and Jackson made it fast to his bow. A radio was passed over. Jackson was surprised to find that it worked. In minutes the cutter was making way for Nova Scotia with the *Carla Mia* in tow, her bow held high by the ship's wake, her transom deep in the water. A relieved Jackson was already making plans for repairing his boat and for a third attempt to complete what he'd started out to do – to singlehand the *Carla Mia* across the Atlantic Ocean.

The tow lasted all that day and night, and during a storm the following night both boats docked in Shelburne, on the lower southeastern shore of Nova Scotia. The *Daring's* first officer, Joe McKenna, and her number two officer, Lloyd Green, were marvelous hosts. Jackson was invited to board the *Daring*, where he was allowed to shower and freshen up, and dine. Back aboard his boat, he rolled into a bunk for a long-needed sleep. It was not to be. Royal Northwest Mounted Police hailed him from the dock. He must come to headquarters and make a telephone report to air search headquarters in Halifax and in New York. These took time, absorbing the remaining hours in that day.

The following daylight found the skipper of the *Carla Mia* searching for a boatyard to repair the ketch. Taken in hand by the mayor of Shelburne, Bill Cox, Jackson was shown more Canadian hospitality. Cox, a member of the Harley Cox & Sons Boatyard in Shelburne, arranged to have the repairs made.

Although Jackson felt fortunate in having received what he termed marvelous cordialities and assistance from the Nova Scotians, he was, by now, also seeing a darker side of fortune. Everything, until now, had worked against him. It seemed obvious that someone, something, as he had feared, was trying to tell him something. And Jackson began to have strong doubts about the solo crossing. Should he chance it? While the repairs were being made to the boat, news agencies and the yacht club learned of Jackson's arrival. Fearing what receptions – further human associations – might do to his resolve, Jackson, as soon as his boat was ready, gritted his teeth and cast off again.

"They were magnificent," he later said of his Canadian hosts, "and I didn't want to disappoint them. Up to this point everything seemed to be against this trip, as though even the Lord was trying to tell me I shouldn't continue, that I should turn back. There were reporters and welcoming yachts coming, and I knew that if I didn't get out of there then, the human contact might have a negative effect on my resolve. I was determined to get out of there and on my way. I waved to everyone, and I called, 'I'll see you again, wish me well!!!' The boat horns sounded and people on them and on the docks cheered as I sailed past."

Still waving farewell, Jackson guided the *Carla Mia* out to sea. He set his course for that point where the sailboat had become disabled, making excellent progress all through a beautiful night. After a wonderful day, the first gale came up and, in Jackson's words, "Blew like hell." When that one subsided, it was followed almost immediately by another, and the notorious Atlantic began spewing its wrath on the *Carla Mia* and her undaunted captain. Storm after storm pounded them unmercifully, day and night, for a month.

"It was cold," Jackson later recalled the battering to which he and the boat had been subjected. "We were wet all the time; me and the boat. The boat looked like a submarine, green water sloshing over the deck, the cockpit, washing over everything, my feet, my hands, down the back of my neck, even though I had on hooded foul weather gear. My skin died, it was so wet all the time. It fell off my hands in patches, from my feet, too, and from my bottom. And cold? I wore wool gloves, a wool stocking hat, and wool longjohns. I had on a wool turtleneck sweater next to my skin, and two more wool sweaters with a wool hunting shirt over them. And I had on foul weather gear. And I still froze."

The *Carla Mia* was in constant violent motion, and the steering vane, so long suspect and undependable, was, by this time, useless. Jackson was forced to remain at the helm, for without guidance the ketch would have quartered into the wind and been pushed back toward the coast of North America. His single-handed passage could have been a beautiful experience. It could have been a pleasant thirty-day sail, with plenty of sun, gentle swells and moderate winds. But Jackson had few such days. During the entire voyage, he had only three clear twilights during which he could take star sights by which to navigate. It was a discouraging situation. The skipper of the *Carla Mia* later reflected on it in this manner:

"Out of sixty-one days you'd expect that I would have at least half of them where I would have a clear sky, when the sun could be seen falling below the horizon, when I could get a clear shot of the horizon. My log will show my almost total dependence on running sun sights."

THE MIGHTY ATLANTIC OFF THE STERN OF THE *CARLA MIA*

Relentlessly, the gales continued. The seas rose threateningly around the *Carla Mia*. In twenty to thirty foot seas, and in winds at forty-five to fifty knots, the little ketch gallantly held her own under sail. As the intensity of the gales increased, Jackson had to lower sail.

"Then you are no longer in control of your boat," he said in recollection of those frenzied hours. "And so you have to go below. You're sitting down there in the forepeak, wedged into the sail bags, and duffel bags, just so you won't get bounced around. And while you're helpless, and you're watching out of the portholes, and you see those waves racing past you, and banging the boat and tossing it around – at a time like that, there's no way you can avoid asking yourself certain questions. And you pause, wondering if you're being punished, if what you're going through is a penalty for not having been a better person, for not having been more religious."

When it occurred to him to ask the intervention of God to help him, Jackson was beset by doubts that he, as an individual, had that right. He had by this time found a great humility, and had come to recognize his insignificance. He remembered that he was suffering alone, as a mere individual, while in the ranks of humanity the world over, innocents were dying in great numbers. As though in answer to his thoughts the maddening gales at last abated, and by contrast, were replaced with a calm that afforded the *Carla Mia* little or no wind. Jackson had been blown off course far enough south to make an Azores landing an attractive subject for thought. He lacked charts of that area, and decided it would be unwise. Besides that, he scolded himself, the Azores were not in his plan.

Becalmed, then, the sailboat going no place, her captain began experiencing a problem not uncommon to singlehanders: hallucinations. Fortunately, Jackson was aware that this was a probability.

"But I became convinced that I was totally thwarted on this trip, and I was again thinking in terms of some evil presence out there in the sea, blocking me," he said. He began experiencing an agonizing loneliness, and with it he became morose and impatient for his voyage to end. It had lost all its attraction, its charm and romance, and he began seeing himself as another ancient mariner, sailing forever on an endless sea. He found himself thinking too often of other singlehanders who, under similar circumstances, ended their lives by simply stepping off their boats into the sea. He repeated to himself, "I won't do that. No matter what, I won't give up. I'll go down with this boat, but I won't give up."

He was sure that he did not want to step off the *Carla Mia* into the Atlantic. He drew an analogy to height, to being atop a tall building and knowing the impulse to step off it, and that he needed only to turn his back to break the spell. This helped, yet he still knew a real fear that he could lose control of himself and end his anguish in that manner. He kept telling himself that if he did, once in the water he would be unable to change his mind, that his boat would sail away without him. And to himself he reiterated, "I won't, I won't. Whatever happens, I won't."

Time passed slowly and Jackson yearned for a cigarette, a smoke. He had been at sea for so many days his supply by this time was exhausted. He wished desperately for the company of the land bird that had taken refuge aboard his boat a couple days out of Nova Scotia. The bird had remained with him, sharing his food and water, before it flew aloft one day and disappeared.

He was running low on water. The crew of a passing trawler had given him some to replenish his

**LAND BIRD RODE OUT A GALE
OFF THE COAST OF NOVA SCOTIA**

supply, but it seemed that no amount could last for his never ending journey. Meats and vegetables were still in good supply aboard his boat, but they did him little good; depressed, he had lost the will to eat. Moreover, he had ignored a cardinal rule of the sea, to keep his boat clean and orderly.

While the *Carla Mia* was buffeted by raging seas, her skipper had approached the nights with foreboding. Now, in the doldrums of that same passage, the nights still were not welcome. The moon repeatedly instilled a fear in him. It rose like a huge red light that seemed always to be attacking the man and his sailboat. It would grow larger and larger, Jackson's fear matching it in size until understanding returned, and he knew that it was only the moon again.

By this time, his weight was down by forty pounds. He was haggard, gaunt, and his clothes hung large and heavily on him. There were moments, especially at night, when he knew he would never again see land, or another human being, and that he would surely die alone at sea. Whatever demon was out there, obstructing the realization of his dream, had succeeded. Mornings were welcome. About four o'clock his spirits lifted, he would then be anxious for the break of day. Finally, a whisp of wind moved the *Carla Mia*.

Earlier gales had blown the boat sufficiently off course to prompt Jackson to change his port of call. He would not sail to Hampton, England. Unseasonal easterlies hampered his progress there. He would sail to Ireland, and he set a course for Cork. In the process, he noted that an Omega navigation system overlay on one chart revealed the presence, twenty-eight miles off the Irish coast, of two off-shore oil rigs. He sent the bow of the *Carla Mia* in their direction.

Was it two or three days now that Jackson had been out of drinking water? He couldn't remember. He was sick and despondent. For days, weeks, he had

GETTING A FIX

been without sleep, because of the broken steering vane. He was on the verge of collapse. His hands, feet and buttocks were raw. And he was starved for human companionship. On the fifth day of September, Jackson saw a tiny spot on the horizon. He studied it with his binoculars. It was an offshore oil rig. A great joy surged through his body. He was nearing land, and, by golly, his navigation was still perfect. His spirits soared, and he was pleased with himself.

The skipper of the *Carla Mia* brought his small craft close to the oil rig. The workers atop it waved and cheered as man and boat passed. Jackson waved back – violently. At last he was communicating with humans, those people up on the rig. He laughed and waved some more, and he jumped up and down for joy. Two hours later the exuberant skipper of the *Carla Mia* could make out the profile of the green hills of Ireland.

After his arrival in Ireland, Jackson was undecided about the CARLA MIA. Vowing that he would never again attempt such a sea voyage, he was not, however, prepared to divest himself of his boat. He put the CARLA MIA in storage and took a plane back to the U.S. and his job at Indiana University.

Without fanfare, in the spring of 1981, he returned to Ireland to sail the CARLA MIA home. Plotting a course south past Spain to the Canary Islands, he hoped to catch the fair trade winds from there to Florida. It was not to be.

On May 10, 1981, pieces of the CARLA MIA were found along the Spanish coast. The dinghy, that had played such an important role in Jackson's Atlantic crossing, and its outboard motor, were not found in the wreckage.

It was presumed W. Carl Jackson had lost his life at sea.

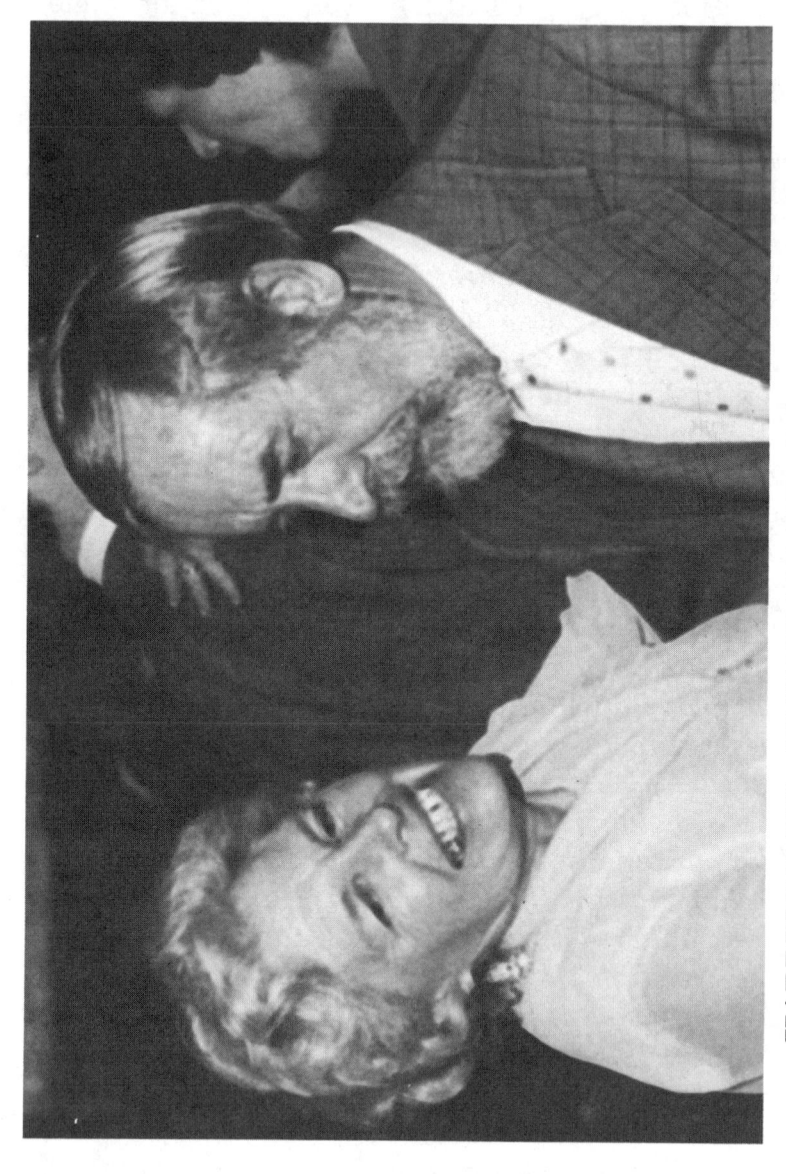

HAPPIER DAYS – ELISABETH AND CARL JACKSON

ECHOES OF JOURNEYS PAST

To order additional copies please fill out the coupon below and mail it to:

>Reunion Books
>3949 Old SR 446
>Bloomington, IN 47401
>Or Call 812-336-8403

Please send me ____ copies of *Echoes of Journeys Past* at $10.50 each, plus 5% tax plus $2.00 shipping and handling.

The Reunion Trilogy, *G'bye My Honey*, *Precious Rascal*, and *Ol' Sam Payton* are available at $9.50 per book, as is *Laughing All The Way with Larry Incollingo*.

MAIL SPECIAL: Any three books $30, tax and shipping included.

My Name: _____

My Address: _____

My City, State, Zip: _____

List Title(s) _____

Check Enclosed: _____

Signature: _____

SEND A GIFT COPY TO A FRIEND.